The Wise Woman

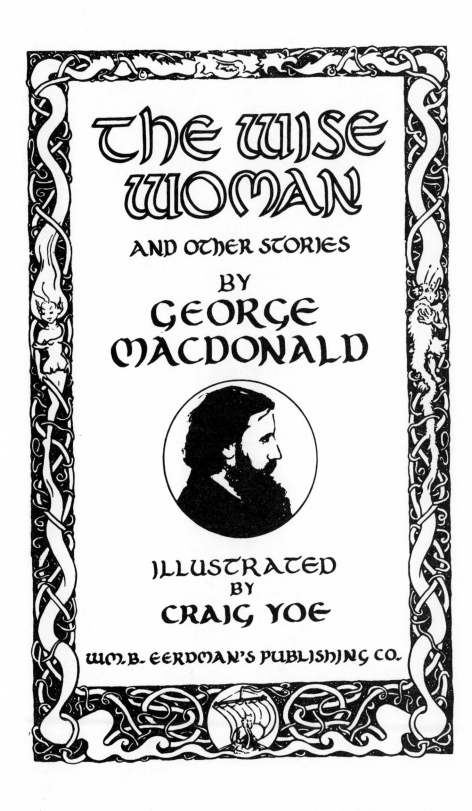

THE WISE WOMAN

AND OTHER STORIES

BY
GEORGE MACDONALD

ILLUSTRATED
BY
CRAIG YOE

WM. B. EERDMAN'S PUBLISHING CO.

©1980 Wm. B. Eerdmans Publishing Co.

Illustrations © 1980 Craig Yoe

This edition published in 2000 by
Wm. B. Eerdmans Publishing Co.
255 Jefferson Ave. S.E., Grand Rapids, Michigan 49503 /
P.O. Box 163, Cambridge CB3 9PU U.K.

Printed in the United States of America

08 07 06 05 04 03   16 15 14 13 12 11

ISBN 0-8028-1860-9

www.eerdmans.com

CONTENTS

ILLUSTRATIONS

The story-title decoration is based on an anagram George MacDonald invented from the letters of his name. It was adopted as a family emblem.

"IT must be more than thirty years ago that I bought . . . *Phantastes*. A few hours later I knew I had crossed a great frontier. . . . What it actually did to me was to convert, even to baptise, my imagination."

In those words C. S. Lewis, creator of the Narnia Chronicles, reported his discovery of George MacDonald, one of the nineteenth-century innovators of modern fantasy. Thanks in part to Lewis's appreciation—"I regarded him as my master"—MacDonald came to influence not only Lewis himself but that circle of Lewis's friends in Oxford who called themselves the Inklings. Included were Charles Williams and—more famously—J. R. R. Tolkien, who has paid his own tribute to the "power and beauty" of MacDonald's accomplishment.

George MacDonald was born in 1824, five years later than Queen Victoria; he died four years after her, in 1905. His birthplace was Huntly, Aberdeenshire, in Northwest Scotland, and his Scottish background shows through his work, in its kindly but unsentimental astringency and its love of the commonplace, even more clearly than does the Victorian world in which he later moved as a resident of London. In 1840 he entered Kings College at Aberdeen, and ten years later he became clergyman to a chapel at Arundel, a position he left in 1853 to begin what was to be a long career as highly respected writer, lecturer, and preacher. Among his literary friends were Carlyle, Tennyson, William Morris, and Lewis Carroll. In 1872 he travelled on a spectacularly successful lecture tour of the United States, where he was hailed by the popular press and saw such prominent men of letters as Whittier and Emerson.

MacDonald wrote a number of conventional Victorian novels, modestly successful in his own time but of interest now largely as period pieces. It is for his entrancing fantasy that MacDonald is justly revered today by an enthusiastic and growing readership. These fantasy works include the adult "Faerie Romances" *Phantastes* and *Lilith* and three full-length children's classics: *At the Back of the North Wind, The Princess and the Goblin*, and *The Princess and Curdie*.

Much of MacDonald's best fantasy writing, however, is found in his shorter stories, which in his lifetime were published in such collections as *Adela Cathcart* (1864) and *The Gifts of the Child Christ, and Other Tales* (1882). In the present volume and its companion volumes in THE FANTASY STORIES OF GEORGE MACDONALD, editor Glenn Sadler has compiled a complete edition of MacDonald's shorter works, newly illustrated by artists Craig and Janet Yoe.

"I do not write," MacDonald once said, "for children, but for the childlike, whether of five, or fifty, or seventy-five." Here, then, for the childlike of all ages, is a collection of fairy tales and stories certain to delight both confirmed MacDonald readers and those about to meet him for the first time.

THE WISE WOMAN, OR THE LOST PRINCESS: A DOUBLE STORY

I

HERE was a certain country where things used to go rather oddly. For instance, you could never tell whether it was going to rain or hail, or whether or not the milk was going to turn sour. It was impossible to say whether the next baby would be a boy, or a girl, or even, after he was a week old, whether he would wake sweet-tempered or cross.

In strict accordance with the peculiar nature of this country of uncertainties, it came to pass one day, that in the midst of a shower of rain that might well be called golden, seeing the sun, shining as it fell, turned all its drops into molten topazes, and every drop was good for a grain of golden corn, or a yellow cowslip, or a buttercup, or a dandelion at least;—while this spendid rain was falling, I say, with a musical patter upon the great leaves of the horse-chestnuts, which hung like Vandyke collars about the necks of the creamy, red-spotted blossoms, and on the leaves of the sycamores, looking as if they had blood in their veins, and on a multitude of flowers, of which some

Serialized under the title "A Double Story" in *Good Things* (1874); also published as "Princess Rosamond" and "The Lost Princess" (1895).

1

stood up and boldly held out their cups to catch their share, while others cowered down, laughing, under the soft patting blows of the heavy warm drops;— while this lovely rain was washing all the air clean from the motes, and the bad odors, and the poison-seeds that had escaped from their prisons during the long drought;—while it fell, splashing and sparkling, with a hum, and a rush, and a soft clashing—but stop! I am stealing, I find, and not that only, but with clumsy hands spoiling what I steal:—

"O Rain! with your dull twofold sound,
The clash hard by, and the murmur all round:"

—there! take it, Mr. Coleridge;—while, as I was saying, the lovely little rivers whose fountains are the clouds, and which cut their own channels through the air, and make sweet noises rubbing against their banks as they hurry down and down, until at length they are pulled up on a sudden, with a musical plash, in the very heart of an odorous flower, that first gasps and then sighs up a blissful scent, or on the bald head of a stone that never says, Thank you;—while the very sheep felt it blessing them, though it could never reach their skins through the depth of their long wool, and the veriest hedgehog—I mean the one with the longest spikes—came and spiked himself out to impale as many of the drops as he could;— while the rain was thus falling, and the leaves, and the flowers, and the sheep, and the cattle, and the hedgehog, were all busily receiving the golden rain, something happened. It was not a great battle, nor an earthquake, nor a coronation, but something more important than all those put together. *A baby-girl was born*; and her father was a king; and her mother was a queen; and her uncles and aunts were princes and princesses; and her first-cousins were dukes and duchesses; and not one of her second-cousins was less than a marquis or marchioness, or of their third-cousins less than an earl or countess: and below a countess they did not care to count. So the little girl was Somebody; and yet for all that, strange to say, the first thing she did was to cry. I told you it was a strange country.

As she grew up, everybody about her did his best to convince her that she was Somebody; and the girl herself was so easily persuaded of it that she quite forgot that anybody had even told her so, and took it for a fundamental, innate, primary, first-born, self-evident, necessary, and incontrovertible idea and principle that *she was Somebody*. And far be it from me to deny it. I will even go so far as to assert that in this odd country there was a huge number of Somebodies. Indeed, it was one of its oddities that every boy and girl in it was rather too ready to think he or she was Somebody; and the worst of it was that the princess never thought of there being more than one Somebody—and that was herself.

Far away to the north in the same country, on the side of a bleak hill, where a horse chestnut or a sycamore was never seen, where were no meadows rich with buttercups, only steep, rough, breezy slopes, covered with dry prickly furze and its flowers of red gold, or moister, softer broom with its flowers of yellow gold, and great sweeps of purple heather, mixed with bilberries, and crowberries, and cranberries—no, I am all wrong: there was nothing out yet but a few furze-blossoms; the rest were all waiting behind their doors till they were called; and no full, slow-gliding river with meadow-sweet along its oozy banks, only a little brook here and there, that dashed past without a moment to say, "How do you do?"—there (would you believe it?) while the same cloud that was dropping down golden rain all about the queen's new

3

baby was dashing huge fierce handfuls of hail upon the hills, with such force that they flew spinning off the rocks and stones, went burrowing in the sheep's wool, stung the cheeks and chin of the shepherd with their sharp spiteful little blows, and made his dog wink and whine as they bounded off his hard wise head, and long sagacious nose; only, when they dropped plump down the chimney, and fell hissing in the fire, they caught it then, for the clever little fire soon sent them up the chimney again, a good deal swollen, and harmless enough for a while, there (what do you think?) among the hailstones, and the heather, and the cold mountain air, another little girl was born, whom the shepherd her father, and shepherdess her mother, and a good many of her kindred too, thought Somebody. She had not an uncle or an aunt that was less than a shepherd or dairymaid, not a cousin that was less than a farm-laborer, not a second-cousin that was less than a grocer, and they did not count farther. And yet (would you believe it?) she too cried the very first thing. It *was* an odd country! And, what is still more surprising, the shepherd and shepherdess and the dairymaids and the laborers were not a bit wiser than the king and the queen and the dukes and the marquises and the earls; for they too, one and all, so constantly taught the little woman that she was Somebody, that she also forgot that there were a great many more Somebodies besides herself in the world.

It was, indeed, a peculiar country, very different from ours—so different, that my reader must not be too much surprised when I add the amazing fact, that most of its inhabitants, instead of enjoying the things they had, were always wanting the things they had not, often even the things it was least likely they ever could have. The grown men and women being like this, there is no reason to be further astonished that the Princess Rosamond—the name her parents gave her because it means *Rose of the World*—should grow up like them, wanting every thing she could and every thing she couldn't have. The things she could have were a great many too many, for her foolish parents always gave her what they could; but still there remained a few things they couldn't give her, for they were only a common king and queen. They could and did give her a lighted candle when she cried for it, and managed by much care that she should not burn her fingers or set her frock on fire; but when she cried for the moon, that they could not give her. They did the worst thing possible, instead, however; for they pretended to do what they could not. They got her a thin disc of brilliantly polished silver, as near the size of the moon as they could agree upon; and, for a time she was delighted.

But, unfortunately, one evening she made the discovery that her moon was a little peculiar, inasmuch as she could not shine in the dark. Her nurse happened to snuff out the candles as she was playing with it; and instantly came a shriek of rage, for her moon had vanished. Presently, through the opening of the curtains, she caught sight of the real moon, far away in the sky, and shining quite calmly, as if she had been there all the time; and her rage increased to such a degree that if it had not passed off in a fit, I do not know what might have come of it.

As she grew up it was still the same, with this difference, that not only must she have every thing, but she got tired of every thing almost as soon as she had it. There was an accumulation of things in her nursery and schoolroom and bedroom that was perfectly appalling. Her mother's wardrobes were almost useless to her, so packed were they with things of which she never took any notice. When she was five years old, they gave her a splendid gold repeater, so close set with diamonds and rubies, that the back was just one crust of gems. In one of her little tempers, as they called her hideously ugly rages, she dashed it against the back of the chimney, after which it never gave a single tick; and some of the diamonds went to the ash-pit. As she grew older still, she became fond of animals, not in a way that brought them much pleasure, or herself much satisfaction. When angry, she would beat them, and try to pull them to pieces, and as soon as she became a little used to them, would neglect them altogether. Then, if they could, they would run away, and she was furious. Some white mice, which she had ceased feeding altogether, did so; and soon the palace was swarming with white mice. Their red eyes might be seen glowing, and their white skins gleaming, in every dark corner; but when it came to the king's finding a nest of them in his second-best crown, he was angry and ordered them to be drowned. The princess heard of it, however, and raised such a clamor, that there they were left until they should run away of themselves; and the poor king had to wear his best crown every day till then. Nothing that was the princess's property, whether she cared for it or not, was to be meddled with.

Of course, as she grew, she grew worse; for she never tried to grow better. She became more and more peevish and fretful every day—dissatisfied not only with what she had, but with all that was around her, and constantly wishing things in general to be different. She found fault with every thing and everybody, and all that happened, and grew more and more disagreeable to every one who had to do with her. At last, when she had nearly killed her nurse, and had all but succeeded in hanging herself, and was miserable from morning to night, her parents thought it time to do something.

A long way from the palace, in a heart of a deep wood of pine-trees, lived a wise woman. In some countries she would have been called a witch; but that would have been a mistake, for she never did any thing wicked, and had more power than any witch could have. As her fame was spread through all the country, the king heard of her; and thinking she might perhaps be able to suggest something, sent for her. In the dead of the night, lest the princess should know it, the king's messenger brought into the palace a tall woman, muffled from head to foot in a cloak of black cloth. In the presence of both their Majesties, the king, to do her honor, requested her to sit; but she declined, and stood waiting to hear what they had to say. Nor had she to wait long, for almost instantly they began to tell her the dreadful trouble they were in with their only child; first the king talking, then the queen interposing with some yet more dreadful fact, and at times both letting out a torrent of words together, so anxious were they to show the wise woman that their perplexity was real, and their daughter a very terrible one. For a long while there appeared no sign of approaching pause. But the wise woman stood patiently folded in her black cloak, and listened without word or motion. At length silence fell; for they had talked themselves tired, and could not think of any thing more to add to the list of their child's enormities.

After a minute, the wise woman unfolded her arms; and her cloak dropping open in front, disclosed a garment made of a strange stuff, which an old poet who knew her well has thus described: —

"All lilly white, withoutten spot or pride,

That seemd like silke and silver woven neare;

But neither silke nor silver therin did appeare."

7

"How very badly you have treated her!" said the wise woman. "Poor child!"

"Treated her badly?" gasped the king.

"She is a very wicked child," said the queen, and both glared with indignation.

"Yes, indeed!" returned the wise woman. "She is very naughty indeed, and that she must be made to feel; but it is half your fault too."

"What!" stammered the king. "Haven't we given her every mortal thing she wanted?"

"Surely," said the wise woman; "what else could have all but killed her? You should have given her a few things of the other sort. But you are far too dull to understand me."

"You are very polite," remarked the king, with royal sarcasm on his thin, straight lips.

The wise woman made no answer beyond a deep sigh; and the king and queen sat silent also in their anger, glaring at the wise woman. The silence lasted again for a minute, and then the wise woman folded her cloak around her, and her shining garment vanished like the moon when a great cloud comes over her. Yet another minute passed and the silence endured, for the smouldering wrath of the king and queen choked the channels of their speech. Then the wise woman turned her back on them, and so stood. At this, the rage of the king broke forth; and he cried to the queen, stammering in his fierceness,—

"How should such an old hag as that teach Rosamond good manners? She knows nothing of them herself! Look how she stands!—actually with her back to us."

At the word the wise woman walked from the room. The great folding doors fell to behind her; and the same moment the king and queen were quarrelling like apes as to which of them was to blame for her departure. Before their altercation was over, for it lasted till the early morning, in rushed Rosamond, clutching in her hand a poor little white rabbit, of which she was very fond, and from which, only because it would not come to her when she called it, she was pulling handfuls of fur in the attempt to tear the squealing, pink-eared, red-eyed thing to pieces.

"Rosa, Rosamond!" cried the queen; whereupon Rosamond threw the rabbit in her mother's face. The king started up in a fury, and ran to seize her. She darted shrieking from the room. The king rushed after her; but, to his amazement, she was nowhere to be seen: the huge hall was empty.—No: just outside the door, close to the threshold, with her back to it, sat the figure of the wise woman, muffled in her dark cloak, with her head bowed over her knees. As the king stood looking at her, she rose slowly, crossed the hall, and walked away down the marble staircase. The king called to her; but she never turned her head, or gave the least sign that she heard him. So quietly did she pass down the wide marble stair, that the king was all but persuaded he had seen only a shadow gliding across the white steps.

For the princess, she was nowhere to be found. The queen went into hysterics; and the rabbit ran away. The king sent out messengers in every direction, but in vain.

In a short time the palace was quiet—as quiet as it used to be before the princess was born. The king and queen cried a little now and then, for the hearts of parents were in that country strangely fashioned; and yet I am afraid the first movement of those very hearts would have been a jump of terror if the ears above them had heard the voice of Rosamond in one of the corridors. As for the rest of the household, they could not have made up a single tear amongst them. They thought, whatever it might be for the princess, it was, for every one else, the best thing

So quietly did the wise woman pass down the stair,
that the king was all but persuaded he had seen only a shadow.

that could have happened; and as to what had become of her, if their heads were puzzled, their hearts took no interest in the question. The lord-chancellor alone had an idea about it, but he was far too wise to utter it.

II

HE fact, as is plain, was, that the princess had disappeared in the folds of the wise woman's cloak. When she rushed from the room, the wise woman caught her to her bosom and flung the black garment around her. The princess struggled wildly, for she was in fierce terror, and screamed as loud as choking fright would permit her; but her father, standing in the door, and looking down upon the wise woman, saw never a movement of the cloak, so tight was she held by her captor. He was indeed aware of a most angry crying, which reminded him of his daughter; but it sounded to him so far away, that he took it for the passion of some child in the street, outside the palace-gates. Hence, unchallenged, the wise woman carried the princess down the marble stairs, out at the palace-door, down a great flight of steps outside, across a paved court, through the brazen gates, along half-roused streets where people were opening their shops, through the huge gates of the city, and out into the wide road, vanishing northwards; the princess struggling and screaming all the time, and the wise woman holding her tight. When at length she was too tired to struggle or scream any more, the wise woman unfolded her cloak, and set her down; and the princess saw the light and opened her swollen eyelids. There was nothing in sight that she had ever seen before. City and palace had disappeared. They were upon a wide road going straight on, with a ditch on each side of it, that behind them

11

widened into the great moat surrounding the city. She cast up a terrified look into the wise woman's face, that gazed down upon her gravely and kindly. Now the princess did not in the least understand kindness. She always took it for a sign either of partiality or fear. So when the wise woman looked kindly upon her, she rushed at her, butting with her head like a ram: but the folds of the cloak had closed around the wise woman; and, when the princess ran against it, she found it hard as the cloak of a bronze statue, and fell back upon the road with a great bruise on her head. The wise woman lifted her again, and put her once more under the cloak, where she fell asleep, and where she awoke again only to find that she was still being carried on and on.

When at length the wise woman again stopped and set her down, she saw around her a bright moonlit night, on a wide heath, solitary and houseless. Here she felt more frightened than before; nor was her terror assuaged when, looking up, she saw a stern immovable countenance, with cold eyes fixedly regarding her. All she knew of the world being derived from nursery-tales, she concluded that the wise woman was an ogress, carrying her home to eat her.

I have already said that the princess was, at this time of her life, such a low-minded creature, that severity had greater influence over her than kindness. She understood terror better far than tenderness. When the wise woman looked at her thus, she fell on her knees, and held up her hands to her, crying,—

"Oh, don't eat me! don't eat me!"

Now this being the best *she* could do, it was a sign she was a low creature. Think of it—to kick at kindness, and kneel from terror. But the sternness on the face of the wise woman came from the same heart and the same feeling as the kindness that had shone from it before. The only thing that could save the princess from her hatefulness, was that she should be made to mind somebody else than her own miserable Somebody.

Without saying a word, the wise woman reached down her hand, took one of Rosamond's, and, lifting her to her feet, led her along through the moonlight. Every now and then a gush of obstinacy would well up in the heart of the princess, and she would give a great ill-tempered tug, and pull her hand away; but then the wise woman would gaze down upon her with such a look, that she instantly sought again the hand she had rejected, in pure terror lest she should be eaten upon the spot. And so they would walk on again; and when the wind blew the folds of the cloak against the princess, she found them soft as her mother's camel-hair shawl.

After a little while the wise woman began to sing to her, and the princess could not help listening; for the soft wind amongst the low dry bushes of the heath, the rustle of their own steps, and the trailing of the wise woman's cloak, were the only sounds beside. And this is the song she sang: —

> *Out in the cold,*
> *With a thin-worn fold*
> *Of withered gold*
> *Around her rolled,*
> *Hangs in the air the weary moon.*
> *She is old, old, old;*
> *And her bones all cold,*
> *And her tales all told,*
> *And her things all sold,*
> *And she has no breath to croon.*

> *Like a castaway clout,*

She is quite shut out!
She might call and shout,
But no one about
Would ever call back, "Who's there?"
There is never a hut,
Not a door to shut,
Not a footpath or rut,
Long road or short cut,
Leading to anywhere!

She is all alone
Like a dog-picked bone,
The poor old crone!
She fain would groan,
But she cannot find the breath.
She once had a fire,
But she built it no higher,
And only sat nigher
Till she saw it expire,
And now she is cold as death.

She never will smile
All the lonesome while
Oh the mile after mile,
And never a stile!
And never a tree or a stone!
She has not a tear:
Afar and anear
It is all so drear,
But she does not care,
Her heart is as dry as a bone.

None to come near her!
No one to cheer her!
No one to jeer her!
Not a thing to lift and hold!
She is always awake,
But her heart will not break:
She can only quake,
Shiver, and shake:
The old woman is very cold.

As strange as the song, was the crooning wailing tune that the wise woman sung. At the first note almost, you would have thought she wanted to frighten the princess; and so indeed she did. For when people *will* be naughty, they have to be frightened, and they are not expected to like it. The princess grew angry, pulled her hand away, and cried, —

"*You* are the ugly old woman. I hate you!"

Therewith she stood still, expecting the wise woman to stop also, perhaps coax her to go on: if she did, she was determined not to move a step. But the wise woman never even looked about: she kept walking on steadily, the same space as before. Little Obstinate thought for certain she would turn; for she regarded herself as much too precious to be left behind. But on and on the wise woman went, until she had vanished away in the dim moonlight. Then all at once the princess perceived that she was left alone with the moon, looking down on her from the height of her loneliness. She was horribly frightened, and began to run after the wise woman, calling aloud. But the song she had just heard came back to the sound of her own running feet, —

All all alone,
Like a dog-picked bone!

15

and again,—

> *She might call and shout,*
> *And no one about*
> *Would ever call back, "Who's there?"*

and she screamed as she ran. How she wished she knew the old woman's name, that she might call it after her through the moonlight!

But the wise woman had, in truth, heard the first sound of her running feet, and stopped and turned, waiting. What with running and crying, however, and a fall or two as she ran, the princess never saw her until she fell right into her arms—and the same moment into a fresh rage; for as soon as any trouble was over the princess was always ready to begin another. The wise woman therefore pushed her away, and walked on; while the princess ran scolding and storming after her. She had to run till, from very fatigue, her rudeness ceased. Her heart gave way; she burst into tears, and ran on, silently weeping.

A minute more and the wise woman stooped, and lifting her in her arms, folded her cloak around her. Instantly she fell asleep, and slept as soft and as soundly as if she had been in her own bed. She slept till the moon went down; she slept till the sun rose up; she slept till he climbed the topmost sky; she slept till he went down again, and poor old moon came peaking and peering out once more: and all that time the wise woman went walking on and on very fast. And now they had reached a spot where a few fir-trees came to meet them through the moonlight.

At the same time the princess awaked, and popping her head out between the folds of the wise woman's cloak—a very ugly little owlet she looked—saw that they were entering the wood. Now there is something awful about every wood, especially in the moonlight; and perhaps a fir-wood is more awful than other woods. For one thing, it lets a little more light through, rendering the darkness a little more visible, as it were; and then the trees go stretching away up towards the moon, and look as if they cared nothing about the creatures below them—not like the broad trees with soft wide leaves that, in the darkness even, look sheltering. So the princess is not to be blamed that she was very much frightened. She is hardly to be blamed either that, assured the wise woman was an ogress carrying her to her castle to eat her up, she began again to kick and scream violently, as those of my readers who are of the same sort as herself will consider the right and natural thing to do. The wrong in her was this—that she had led such a bad life, that she did not know a good woman when she saw her; took her for one like herself, even after she had slept in her arms.

Immediately the wise woman set her down, and, walking on, within a few paces vanished among the trees. Then the cries of the princess rent the air, but the fir-trees never heeded her; not one of their hard little needles gave a single shiver for all the noise she made. But there were creatures in the forest who were soon quite as much interested in her cries as the fir-trees were indifferent to them. They began to hearken and howl and snuff about, and run hither and thither, and grin with their white teeth, and light up the green lamps in their eyes. In a minute or two a whole army of wolves and hyenas were rushing from all quarters through the pillar-like stems of the fir-trees, to the place where she stood calling them, without knowing it. The noise she made herself, however, prevented her from hearing either their howls or the soft pattering of their many trampling feet as they bounded over the fallen fir needles and cones.

One huge old wolf had outsped the rest—not that

17

he could run faster, but that from experience he could more exactly judge whence the cries came, and as he shot through the wood, she caught sight at last of his lamping eyes coming swiftly nearer and nearer. Terror silenced her. She stood with her mouth open, as if she were going to eat the wolf, but she had no breath to scream with, and her tongue curled up in her mouth like a withered and frozen leaf. She could do nothing but stare at the coming monster. And now he was taking a few shorter bounds, measuring the distance for the one final leap that should bring him upon her, when out stepped the wise woman from behind the very tree by which she had set the princess down, caught the wolf by the throat half-way in his last spring, shook him once, and threw him from her dead. Then she turned towards the princess, who flung herself into her arms, and was instantly lapped in the folds of her cloak.

But now the huge army of wolves and hyenas had rushed like a sea around them, whose waves leaped with hoarse roar and hollow yell up against the wise woman. But she, like a strong stately vessel, moved unhurt through the midst of them. Even as they leaped against her cloak, they dropped and slunk away back through the crowd. Others ever succeeded, and ever in their turn fell, and drew back confounded. For some time she walked on attended and assailed on all sides by the howling pack. Suddenly they turned and swept away, vanishing in the depths of the forest. She neither slackened nor hastened her step, but went walking on as before.

In a little while she unfolded her cloak, and let the princess look out. The firs had ceased; and they were on a lofty height of moorland, stony and bare and dry, with tufts of heather and a few small plants here and there. About the heath, on every side, lay the forest, looking in the moonlight like a cloud; and above the forest, like the shaven crown of a monk, rose the bare moor over which they were walking. Presently, a little way in front of them, the princess espied a white-washed cottage, gleaming in the moon. As they came nearer, she saw that the roof was covered with thatch, over which the moss had grown green. It was a very simple, humble place, not in the least terrible to look at, and yet, as soon as she saw it, her fear again awoke, and always, as soon as her fear awoke, the trust of the princess fell into a dead sleep. Foolish and useless as she might by this time have known it, she once more began kicking and screaming, where-upon, yet once more, the wise woman set her down on the heath, a few yards from the back of the cottage, and saying only, "No one ever gets into my house who does not knock at the door, and ask to come in," disappeared round the corner of the cottage, leaving the princess alone with the moon—two white faces in the cone of the night.

III

HE moon stared at the princess, and the prin-cess stared at the moon; but the moon had the best of it, and the princess began to cry. And now the question was between the moon and the cottage. The princess thought she knew the worst of the moon, and she knew nothing at all about the cottage, there-fore she would stay with the moon. Strange, was it not, that she should have been so long with the wise woman, and yet know *nothing* about that cottage? As for the moon, she did not by any means know the worst of her, or even, that, if she were to fall asleep where she could find her, the old witch would cer-tainly do her best to twist her face.

But she had scarcely sat a moment longer before she was assailed by all sorts of fresh fears. First of

19

all, the soft wind blowing gently through the dry stalks
of the heather and its thousands of little bells raised
a sweet rustling, which the princess took for the hissing of serpents, for you know she had been naughty
for so long that she could not in a great many things
tell the good from the bad. Then nobody could deny
that there, all round about the heath, like a ring of
darkness, lay the gloomy fir-wood, and the princess
knew what it was full of, and every now and then she
thought she heard the howling of its wolves and
hyenas. And who could tell but some of them might
break from their covert and sweep like a shadow
across the heath? Indeed, it was not once nor twice
that for a moment she was fully persuaded she saw
a great beast coming leaping and bounding through
the moonlight to have her all to himself. She did not
know that not a single evil creature dared set foot on
that heath, or that, if one should do so, it would that
instant wither up and cease. If an army of them had
rushed to invade it, it would have melted away on the
edge of it, and ceased like a dying wave.—She even
imagined that the moon was slowly coming neared
and nearer down the sky to take her and freeze her
to death in her arms. The wise woman, too, she felt
sure, although her cottage looked asleep, was watching her at some little window. In this, however, she
would have been quite right, if she had only imagined
enough—namely, that the wise woman was watching
over her from the little window. But after all, somehow, the thought of the wise woman was less frightful than that of any of her other terrors, and at length
she began to wonder whether it might not turn out
that she was no ogress, but only a rude, ill-bred, ty-
rannical, yet on the whole not altogether ill-meaning
person. Hardly had the possibility arisen in her mind,
before she was on her feet: if the woman was any
thing short of an ogress, her cottage must be better

than that horrible loneliness, with nothing in all the world but a stare; and even an ogress had at least the shape and look of a human being.

She darted round the end of the cottage to find the front. But, to her surprise, she came only to another back, for no door was to be seen. She tried the farther end, but still no door. She must have passed it as she ran—but no—neither in gable nor in side was any to be found.

A cottage without a door!—she rushed at it in a rage and kicked at the wall with her feet. But the wall was hard as iron, and hurt her sadly through her gay silken slippers. She threw herself on the heath, which came up to the walls of the cottage on every side, and roared and screamed with rage. Suddenly, however, she remembered how her screaming had brought the horde of wolves and hyenas about her in the forest, and, ceasing at once, lay still, gazing yet again at the moon. And then came the thought of her parents in the palace at home. In her mind's eye she saw her mother sitting at her embroidery with the tears dropping upon it, and her father staring into the fire as if he were looking for her in its glowing caverns. It is true that if they had both been in tears by her side because of her naughtiness, she would not have cared a straw; but now her own forlorn condition somehow helped her to understand their grief at having lost her, and not only a great longing to be back in her comfortable home, but a feeble flutter of genuine love for her parents awoke in her heart as well, and she burst into real tears—soft mournful tears—very different from those of rage and disappointment to which she was so much used. And another very remarkable thing was that the moment she began to love her father and mother, she began to wish to see the wise woman again. The idea of her being an ogress vanished utterly, and she thought of her only as one to take her in from the moon, and the loneliness, and the terrors of the forest-haunted heath, and hide her in a cottage with not even a door for the horrid wolves to howl against.

But the old woman—as the princess called her, not knowing that her real name was the Wise Woman—had told her that she must knock at the door: how was she to do that when there was no door? But again she bethought herself—that, if she could not do all she was told, she could, at least, do a part of it: if she could not knock at the door, she could at least knock—say on the wall, for there was nothing else to knock upon—and perhaps the old woman would hear her, and lift her in by some window. Thereupon, she rose at once to her feet, and picking up a stone, began to knock on the wall with it. A loud noise was the result, and she found she was knocking on the very door itself. For a moment she feared the old woman would be offended, but the next, there came a voice, saying,

"Who is there?"

The princess answered,

"Please, old woman, I did not mean to knock so loud."

To this there came no reply.

Then the princess knocked again, this time with her knuckles, and the voice came again, saying,

"Who is there?"

And the princess answered,

"Rosamond."

Then a second time there was silence. But the princess soon ventured to knock a third time.

"What do you want?" said the voice.

"Oh, please, let me in!" said the princess. "The moon will keep staring at me; and I hear the wolves in the wood."

Then the door opened, and the princess entered.

She looked all around, but saw nothing of the wise woman.

It was a single bare little room, with a white deal table, and a few old wooden chairs, a fire of fir-wood on the hearth, the smoke of which smelt sweet, and a patch of thick-growing heath in one corner. Poor as it was, compared to the grand place Rosamond had left, she felt no little satisfaction as she shut the door, and looked around her. And what with the sufferings and terrors she had left outside, the new kind of tears she had shed, the love she had begun to feel for her parents, and the trust she had begun to place in the wise woman, it seemed to her as if her soul had grown larger of a sudden, and she had left the days of her childishness and naughtiness far behind her. People are so ready to think themselves changed when it is only their mood that is changed! Those who are good-tempered because it is a fine day, will be ill-tempered when it rains: their selves are just the same both days; only in the one case, the fine weather has got into them, in the other the rainy. Rosamond, as she sat warming herself by the glow of the peat-fire, turning over in her mind all that had passed, and feeling how pleasant the change in her feelings was, began by degrees to think how very good she had grown, and how very good she was to have grown good, and how extremely good she must always have been that she was able to grow so very good as she now felt she had grown; and she became so absorbed in her self-admiration as never to notice either that the fire was dying, or that a heap of fire-cones lay in a corner near it. Suddenly, a great wind came roaring down the chimney, and scattered the ashes about the floor; a tremendous rain followed, and fell hissing on the embers; the moon was swallowed up, and there was darkness all about her. Then a flash of lightning, followed by a peal of thunder, so terrified the princess, that she cried aloud for the old woman, but there came no answer to her cry.

Then in her terror the princess grew angry, and saying to herself, "She must be somewhere in the place, else who was there to open the door to me?" began to shout and yell, and call the wise woman all the bad names she had been in the habit of throwing at her nurses. But there came not a single sound in reply.

Strange to say, the princess never thought of telling herself now how naughty she was, though that would surely have been reasonable. On the contrary, she thought she had a perfect right to be angry, for was she not most desperately ill used—and a princess too? But the wind howled on, and the rain kept pouring down the chimney, and every now and then the lightning burst out, and the thunder rushed after it, as if the great lumbering sound could ever think to catch up with the swift light!

At length the princess had again grown so angry, frightened, and miserable, all together, that she jumped up and hurried about the cottage with outstretched arms, trying to find the wise woman. But being in a bad temper always makes people stupid, and presently she struck her forehead such a blow against something—she thought herself it felt like the old woman's cloak—that she fell back—not on the floor, though, but on the patch of heather, which felt as soft and pleasant as any bed in the palace. There, worn out with weeping and rage, she soon fell fast asleep.

She dreamed that she was the old cold woman up in the sky, with no home and no friends, and no nothing at all, not even a picket; wandering, wandering forever, over a desert of blue sand, never to get to anywhere, and never to lie down or die. It was no use stopping to look about her, for what had she to do but for ever look about her as she went on and on and on—never seeing any thing, and never expecting to see any thing! The only shadow of a hope she had was, that she might by slow degrees grow thinner and thinner, until at last she wore away to nothing at all; only alas! She could not detect the least sign that she had yet begun to grow thinner. The hopelessness grew at length so unendurable that she woke with a start. Seeing the face of the wise woman bending over her, she threw her arms around her neck and held up her mouth to be kissed. And the kiss of the wise woman was like the rose-gardens of Damascus.

IV

HE wise woman lifted her tenderly, and washed and dressed her far more carefully than even her nurse. Then she set her down by the fire, and prepared her breakfast. The princess was very hungry, and the bread and milk as good as it could be, so that she thought she had never in her life eaten any thing nicer. Nevertheless, as soon as she began to have enough, she said to herself—

"Ha! I see how it is! The old woman wants to fatten me! That is why she gives me such nice creamy milk. She doesn't kill me now because she's going to kill me then! She *is* an ogress, after all!"

Thereupon she laid down her spoon, and would not eat another mouthful—only followed the basin with longing looks, as the wise woman carried it away.

When she stopped eating, her hostess knew exactly what she was thinking; but it was one thing to understand the princess, and quite another to make the princess understand her: that would require time. For the present she took no notice, but went about the affairs of the house, sweeping the floor, brushing down the cobwebs, cleaning the hearth, dusting the table and chairs, and watering the bed to keep it fresh and alive—for she never had more than one guest at a time, and never would allow that guest to go to sleep upon any thing that had no life in it. All the time she was thus busied, she spoke not a word to the princess, which, with the princess, went to confirm her notion of her purposes. But whatever she might have said would have been only perverted by the princess into yet stronger proof of her evil designs, for a fancy in her own head would outweigh any multitude of facts in another's. She kept staring at the fire, and never looked round to see what the wise woman might be doing.

By and by she came close up to the back of her chair, and said,

"Rosamond!"

But the princess had fallen into one of her sulky moods, and shut herself up with her own ugly Somebody; so she never looked round or even answered the wise woman.

"Rosamond," she repeated, "I am going out. If you are a good girl, that is, if you do as I tell you, I will carry you back to your father and mother the moment I return."

The princess did not take the least notice.

"Look at me, Roasmond," said the wise woman.

But Rosamond never moved—never even shrugged her shoulders—perhaps because they were already up to her ears, and could go no farther.

"I want to help you to do what I tell you," said the wise woman. "Look at me."

Still Rosamond was motionless and silent, saying only to herself,

"I know what she's after! She wants to show me her horrid teeth. But I won't look. I'm not going to be frightened out of my senses to please her."

26

"You had better look, Rosamond. Have you forgotten how you kissed me this morning?"

But Rosamond now regarded that little throb of affection as a momentary weakness into which the deceitful ogress had betrayed her, and almost despised herself for it. She was one of those who the more they are coaxed are the more disagreeable. For such, the wise woman had an awful punishment, but she remembered that the princess had been very ill brought up, and therefore wished to try her with all gentleness first.

She stood silent for a moment, to see what effect her words might have. But Rosamond only said to herself,—

"She wants to fatten and eat me."

And it was such a little while since she had looked into the wise woman's loving eyes, thrown her arms round her neck, and kissed her!

"Well," said the wise woman gently, after pausing as long as it seemed possible she might bethink herself, "I must tell you then without; only whoever listens with her back turned, listens but half, and gets but half the help."

"She wants to fatten me," said the princess.

"You must keep the cottage tidy while I am out. When I come back, I must see the fire bright, the hearth swept, and the kettle boiling; no dust on the table or chairs, the windows clear, the floor clean, and the heather in blossom—which last comes of sprinkling it with water three times a day. When you are hungry, put your hand into that hole in the wall, and you will find a meal."

"She wants to fatten me," said the princess.

"But on no account leave the house till I come back," continued the wise woman, "or you will grievously repent it. Remember what you have already gone through to reach it. Dangers lie all around this

27

cottage of mine, but inside, it is the safest place—in fact the only quite safe place in all the country."

"She means to eat me," said the princess, "and therefore wants to frighten me from running away."

She heard the voice no more. Then, suddenly startled at the thought of being alone, she looked hastily over her shoulder. The cottage was indeed empty of all visible life. It was soundless, too: there was not even a ticking clock or a flapping flame. The fire burned still and smouldering-wise; but it was all the company she had, and she turned again to stare into it.

Soon she began to grow weary of having nothing to do. Then she remembered that the old woman, as she called her, had told her to keep the house tidy.

"The miserable little pig-sty!" she said. "Where's the use of keeping such a hovel clean!"

But in truth she would have been glad of the employment, only just because she had been told to do it, she was unwilling; for there *are* people—however unlikely it may seem—who object to doing a thing for no other reason than that it is required of them.

"I am a princess," she said, "and it is very improper to ask me to do such a thing."

She might have judged it quite as suitable for a princess to sweep away the dust as to sit the centre of a world of dirt. But just because she ought, she wouldn't. Perhaps she feared that if she gave in to doing her duty once, she might have to do it always— which was true enough—for that was the very thing for which she had been specially born.

Unable, however, to feel quite comfortable in the resolve to neglect it, she said to herself, "I'm sure there's time enough for such a nasty job as that!" and sat on, watching the fire as it burned away, the glowing red casting off white flakes, and sinking lower and lower on the hearth.

By and by, merely for want of something to do, she would see what the old woman had left for her in the hole of the wall. But when she put in her hand she found nothing there, except the dust which she ought by this time to have wiped away. Never reflecting that the wise woman had told her she would find food there *when she was hungry*, she flew into one of her furies, calling her a cheat, and a thief, and a liar, and an ugly old witch, and an ogress, and I do not know how many wicked names besides. She raged until she was quite exhausted, and then fell fast asleep on her chair. When she awoke, the fire was out.

By this time she was hungry; but without looking in the hole, she began again to storm at the wise woman, in which labor she would no doubt have once more exhausted herself, had not something white caught her eye: it was the corner of a napkin hanging from the hole in the wall. She bounded to it, and there was a dinner for her of something strangely good—one of her favorite dishes, only better than she had ever tasted it before. This might surely have at least changed her mood towards the wise woman; but she only grumbled to herself that it was as it ought to be, ate up the food, and lay down on the bed, never thinking of fire, or dust, or water for the heather.

The wind began to moan about the cottage, and grew louder and louder, till a great gust came down the chimney, and again scattered the white ashes all over the place. But the princess was by this time fast asleep, and never woke till the wind had sunk to silence. One of the consequences, however, of sleeping when one ought to be awake is waking when one ought to be asleep; and the princess awoke in the black midnight, and found enough to keep her awake. For although the wind had fallen, there was a far more terrible howling than that of the wildest wind all about the cottage. Nor was the howling all; the air was full of strange cries; and everywhere she heard the noise of claws scratching against the house, which seemed all doors and windows, so crowded were the sounds, and from so many directions. All the night long she lay half swooning, yet listening to the hideous noises. But with the first glimmer of morning they ceased.

Then she said to herself, "How fortunate it was that I woke! They would have eaten me up if I had been asleep." The miserable little wretch actually talked as if she had kept them out! If she had done her work in the day, she would have slept through the terrors of the darkness, and awaked fearless; whereas now, she had in the storehouse of her heart a whole harvest of agonies, reaped from the dun fields of the night!

They were neither wolves or hyenas which had caused her such dismay, but creatures of the air, more frightful still, which, as soon as the smoke of the burning fir-wood ceased to spread itself abroad, and the sun was a sufficient distance down the sky, and the lone cold woman was out, came flying and howling about the cottage, trying to get in at every door and window. Down the chimney they would have got, but that at the heart of the fire there always lay a certain fir-cone, which looked like solid gold red-hot, and which, although it might easily get covered up with ashes, so as to be quite invisible, was continually in a glow fit to kindle all the fir-cones in the world; this it was which had kept the horrible birds— some say they have a claw at the tip of every wing-feather—from tearing the poor naughty princess to pieces, and gobbling her up.

When she rose and looked about her, she was dismayed to see what a state the cottage was in. The fire was out, and the windows were all dim with the wings and claws of the dirty birds, while the bed from which she had just risen was brown and withered, and half its purple bells had fallen. But she consoled herself that she could set all to rights in a few min- utes—only she must breakfast first. And, sure enough, there was a basin of the delicious bread and milk ready for her in the hole of the wall!

After she had eaten it, she felt comfortable, and sat for a long time building castles in the air—till she was actually hungry again, without having done an atom of work. She ate again, and was idle again, and ate again. Then it grew dark, and she went trembling to bed, for now she remembered the horrors of the last night. This time she never slept at all, but spent the long hours in grievous terror, for the noises were worse than before. She vowed she would not pass another night in such a hateful, haunted old shed for all the ugly women, witches, and ogresses in the wide world. In the morning, however, she fell asleep, and slept late.

Breakfast was of course her first thought, after which she could not avoid that of work. It made her very miserable, but she feared the consequences of being found with it undone. A few minutes before noon, she actually got up, took her pinafore for a duster, and proceeded to dust the table. But the wood- ashes flew about so, that it seemed useless to at- tempt getting rid of them, and she sat down again to think what was to be done. But there is very little indeed to be done when we will not do that which we have to do.

Her first thought now was to run away at once while the sun was high, and get through the forest before night came on. She fancied she could easily go back the way she had come, and get home to her father's palace. But not the most experienced traveller in the world can ever go back the way the wise woman has brought him.

She got up and went to the door. It was locked! What could the old woman have meant by telling her not to leave the cottage? She was indignant.

The wise woman had meant to make it difficult, but not impossible. Before the princess, however, could find the way out, she heard a hand at the door, and darted in terror behind it. The wise woman opened it, and, leaving it open, walked straight to the hearth. Rosamond immediately slid out, ran a little way, and then laid herself down in the long heather.

V

THE wise woman walked straight up to the hearth, looked at the fire, looked at the bed, glanced round the room, and went up to the table. When she saw the one streak in the thick dust which the princess had left there, a smile, half sad, half pleased, like the sun peeping through a cloud on a rainy day in spring, gleamed over her face. She went at once to the door, and called in a loud voice,

"Rosamond, come to me."

All the wolves and hyenas, fast asleep in the wood, heard her voice, and shivered in their dreams. No wonder then that the princess trembled, and found herself compelled, she could not understand how, to obey the summons. She rose, like the guilty thing she felt, forsook of herself the hiding-place she had chosen, and walked slowly back to the cottage she had left full of the signs of her shame. When she entered, she saw the wise woman on her knees, building up the fire with fir-cones. Already the flame was climbing through the heap in all directions, crackling gently, and sending a sweet aromatic odor through the dusty cottage.

"That is my part of the work," she said, rising. "Now you do yours. But first let me remind you that if you had not put it off, you would have found it not only far easier, but by and by quite pleasant work, much more pleasant than you can imagine now; nor would you have found the time go wearily: you would neither have slept in the day and let the fire out, nor waked at night and heard the howling of the beast-birds. More than all, you would have been glad to see me when I came back; and would have leaped into my arms instead of standing there, looking so ugly and foolish."

As she spoke, suddenly she held up before the princess a tiny mirror, so clear that nobody looking into it could tell what it was made of, or even see it at all—only the thing reflected in it. Rosamond saw a child with dirty fat cheeks, greedy mouth, cowardly eyes—which, not daring to look forward, seemed trying to hide behind an impertinent nose—stooping shoulders, tangled hair, tattered clothes, and smears and stains everywhere. That was what she had made herself. And to tell the truth, she was shocked at the sight, and immediately began, in her dirty heart, to lay the blame on the wise woman, because she had taken her away from her nurses and her fine clothes; while all the time she knew well enough that, close by the heather-bed, was the loveliest little well, just big enough to wash in, the water of which was always springing fresh from the ground and running away through the wall. Beside it lay the whitest of linen towels, with a comb made of mother-of-pearl, and a brush of fir-needles, any one of which she had been far too lazy to use. She dashed the glass out of the wise woman's hand, and there it lay, broken into a thousand pieces!

Without a word, the wise woman stooped, and gathered the fragments—did not leave searching until she had gathered the last atom, and she laid them all carefully, one by one, in the fire, now blazing high on the hearth. Then she stood up and looked at the princess, who had been watching her sulkily.

"Rosamond," she said, with a countenance awful in its sternness, "until you have cleansed this room—"

"She calls it a room!" sneered the princess to herself.

"You shall have no morsel to eat. You may drink of the well, but nothing else you shall have. When the work I set you is done, you will find food in the same place as before. I am going from home again; and again I warn you not to leave the house."

"She calls it a house!—It's a good thing she's going out of it anyhow!" said the princess, turning her back for mere rudeness, for she was one who, even if she liked a thing before, would dislike it the moment any person in authority over her desired her to do it.

When she looked again, the wise woman had vanished.

Thereupon the princess ran at once to the door, and tried to open it; but open it would not. She searched on all sides, but could discover no way of getting out. The windows would not open—at least she could not open them; and the only outlet seemed the chimney, which she was afraid to try because of the fire, which looked angry, she thought, and shot out green flames when she went near it. So she sat down to consider. One may well wonder what room for consideration there was—with all her work lying undone behind her. She sat thus, however, considering, as she called it, until hunger began to sting her, when she jumped up and put her hand as usual in the hole of the wall: there was nothing there. She fell straight into one of her stupid rages; but neither her hunger nor the hole in the wall heeded her rage.

Then, in a burst of self-pity, she fell a-weeping, but neither the hunger nor the hole cared for her tears. The darkness began to come on, and her hunger grew and grew, and the terror of the wild noises of the last night invaded her. Then she began to feel cold, and saw that the fire was dying. She darted to the heap of cones, and fed it. It blazed up cheerily, and she was comforted a little. Then she thought with herself it would surely be better to give in so far, and do a little work, than die of hunger. So catching up a duster, she began upon the table. The dust flew about and nearly choked her. She ran to the well to drink, and was refreshed and encouraged. Perceiving now that it was a tedious plan to wipe the dust from the table on to the floor, whence it would have all to be swept up again, she got a wooden platter, wiped the dust into that, carried it to the fire, and threw it in. But all the time she was getting more and more hungry and, although she tried the hole again and again, it was only to become more and more certain that work she must if she would eat.

At length all the furniture was dusted, and she began to sweep the floor, which, happily, she thought of sprinkling with water, as from the window she had seen them do to the marble court of the palace. That swept, she rushed again to the hole—but still no food! She was on the verge of another rage, when the thought came that she might have forgotten something. To her dismay she found that table and chairs and everything was again covered with dust—not so badly as before, however. Again she set to work, driven by hunger, and drawn by the hope of eating, and yet again, after a second careful wiping, sought the hole. But no! nothing was there for her! What could it mean?

Her asking this question was a sign of progress: it showed that she expected the wise woman to keep

35

her word. Then she bethought her that she had forgotten the household utensils, and the dishes and
plates, some of which wanted to be washed as well
as dusted.

Faint with hunger, she set to work yet again. One
thing made her think of another, until at length she
had cleaned every thing she could think of. Now surely
she must find some food in the hole!

When this time also there was nothing, she began
once more to abuse the wise woman as false and
treacherous;—but ah! there was the bed unwatered!
That was soon amended.—Still no supper! Ah! there
was the hearth unswept, and the fire wanted making
up!—Still no supper! What else could there be? She
was at her wits' end, and in very weariness, not la-
ziness this time, sat down and gazed into the fire.
There, as she gazed, she spied something brilliant,—
shining even, in the midst of the fire: it was the little
mirror all whole again; but little she knew that the
dust which she had thrown into the fire had helped
to heal it. She drew it out carefully, and, looking into
it, saw, not indeed the ugly creature she had seen
there before, but still a very dirty little animal; whereupon she hurried to the well, took off her clothes,
plunged into it, and washed herself clean. Then she
brushed and combed her hair, made her clothes as
tidy as might be, and ran to the hole in the wall: there
was a huge basin of bread and milk!

Never had she eaten any thing with half the relish!
Alas! however, when she had finished, she did not
wash the basin, but left it as it was, revealing how
entirely all the rest had been done only from hunger.
Then she threw herself on the heather, and was fast
asleep in a moment. Never an evil bird came near her
all that night, nor had she so much as one troubled
dream.

In the morning as she lay awake before getting up,

she spied what seemed a door behind the tall eight-day clock that stood silent in the corner.

"Ah!" she thought, "that must be the way out!" and got up instantly. The first thing she did, however, was to go to the hole in the wall. Nothing was there.

"Well, I am hardly used!" she cried aloud. "All that cleaning for the cross old woman yesterday, and this for my trouble,—nothing for breakfast! Not even a crust of bread! Does Mistress Ogress fancy a princess will bear that?"

The poor foolish creature seemed to think that the work of one day ought to serve for the next day too! But that is nowhere the way in the whole universe. How could there be a universe in that case? And even she never dreamed of applying the same rule to her breakfast.

"How good I was all yesterday!" she said, "and how hungry and ill used I am to-day!"

But she would *not* be a slave, and do over again to-day what she had done only last night! *She* didn't care about her breakfast! She might have it no doubt if she dusted all the wretched place again, but she was not going to do that—at least, without seeing first what lay behind the clock!

Off she darted, and putting her hand behind the clock found the latch of a door. It lifted, and the door opened a little way. By squeezing hard, she managed to get behind the clock, and so through the door. But how she stared, when instead of the open heath, she found herself on the marble floor of a large and stately room, lighted only from above. Its walls were strengthened by pilasters, and in every space between was a large picture, from cornice to floor. She did not know what to make of it. Surely she had run all round the cottage, and certainly had seen nothing of this size near it! She forgot that she had also run round what she took for a hay-mow, a peat-stack, and

37

several other things which looked of no consequence in the moonlight.

"So, then," she cried, "the old woman *is* a cheat! I believe she's an ogress, after all, and lives in a palace—though she pretends it's only a cottage, to keep people from suspecting that she eats good little children like me!"

Had the princess been tolerably tractable, she would, by this time, have known a good deal about the wise woman's beautiful house, whereas she had never till now got farther than the porch. Neither was she at all in its innermost places now.

But, king's daughter as she was, she was not a little daunted when, stepping forward from the recess of the door, she saw what a great lordly hall it was. She dared hardly look to the other end, it seemed so far off: so she began to gaze at the things near her, and the pictures first of all, for she had a great liking for pictures. One in particular attracted her attention. She came back to it several times, and at length stood absorbed in it.

A blue summer sky, with white fleecy clouds floating beneath it, hung over a hill green to the very top, and alive with streams darting down its sides toward the valley below. On the face of the hill strayed a flock of sheep feeding, attended by a shepherd and two dogs. A little way apart, a girl stood with bare feet in a brook, building across it a bridge of rough stones. The wind was blowing her hair back from her rosy face. A lamb was feeding close beside her; and a sheepdog was trying to reach her hand to lick it.

"Oh, how I wish I were that little girl!" said the princess aloud. "I wonder how it is that some people are made to be so much happier than others! If I were that little girl, no one would ever call me naughty."

She gazed and gazed at the picture. It is the real country, with a real hill, and a real little girl upon it.

I shall soon see whether this isn't another of the old witch's cheats!"

She went close up to the picture, lifted her foot, and stepped over the frame.

"I am free, I am free!" she exclaimed; and she felt the wind upon her cheek.

The sound of a closing door struck on her ear. She turned—and there was a blank wall, without door or window, behind her. The hill with the sheep was before her, and she set out at once to reach it.

Now, if I am asked how this could be, I can only answer, that it was a result of the interaction of things outside and things inside, of the wise woman's skill, and the silly child's folly. If this does not satisfy my questioner, I can only add, that the wise woman was able to do far more wonderful things than this.

VI

EANTIME the wise woman was busy as she always was; and her business now was with the child of the shepherd and shepherdess, away in the north. Her name was Agnes.

Her father and mother were poor, and could not give her many things. Rosamond would have utterly despised the rude, simple playthings she had. Yet in one respect they were of more value far than hers: the king bought Rosamond's with his money; Agnes's father made hers with his hands.

And while Agnes had but few things—not seeing many things about her, and not even knowing that there were many things anywhere, she did not wish for many things, and was therefore neither covetous nor avaricious.

She played with the toys her father made her, and thought them the most wonderful things in the world—windmills, and little crooks, and waterwheels, and sometimes lambs made all of wood, and dolls made out of the leg-bones of sheep, which her mother dressed for her; and of such playthings she was never tired. Sometimes, however, she preferred playing with stones, which were plentiful, and flowers, which were few, or the brooks that ran down the hill, of which, although they were many, she could only play with one at a time, and that, indeed, troubled her a little—or live lambs that were not all wool, or the sheep-dogs, which were very friendly with her, and the best of playfellows, as she thought, for she had no human ones to compare them with. Neither was she greedy after nice things, but content, as well she might be, with the homely food provided for her. Nor was she by nature particularly self-willed or disobedient; she generally did what her father and mother wished, and believed what they told her. But by degrees they had spoiled her; and this was the way: they were so proud of her that they always repeated every thing she said, and told every thing she did, even when she was present; and so full of admiration of their child were they, that they wondered and laughed at and praised things in her which in another child would never have struck them as the least remarkable, and some things even which would in another have disgusted them altogether. Impertinent and rude things done by *their* child they thought *so* clever! laughing at them as something quite marvellous; her commonplace speeches were said over again as if they had been the finest poetry; and the pretty ways which every moderately good child has were extolled as if the result of her excellent taste, and the choice of her judgment and will. They would even say sometimes that she ought not to hear her own praises for fear it should make her vain, and then whisper them behind their hands, but so loud that she could not fail to hear every word. The consequence was that she soon came to believe—so soon, that she could not recall the time when she did not believe, as the most absolute fact in the universe, that she was *Somebody*; that is, she became most immoderately conceited.

Now as the least atom of conceit is a thing to be ashamed of, you may fancy what she was like with such a quantity of it inside her! At first it did not show itself outside in any very active form; but the wise woman had been to the cottage, and had seen her sitting alone, with such a smile of self-satisfaction upon her face as would have been quite startling to her, if she had ever been startled at any thing; for through that smile she could see lying at the root of it the worm that made it. For some smiles are like the ruddiness of certain apples, which is owing to a centipede, or other creeping thing, coiled up at the heart of them. Only her worm had a face and shape the very image of her own; and she looked so simpering, and mawkish, and self-conscious, and silly, that she made the wise woman feel rather sick.

Not that the child was a fool. Had she been, the wise woman would have only pitied and loved her, instead of feeling sick when she looked at her. She had very fair abilities, and were she once but made humble, would be capable not only of doing a good deal in time, but of beginning at once to grow to no end. But, if she were not made humble, her growing would be to a mass of distorted shapes all huddled together; so that, although the body she now showed might grow up straight and well-shaped and comely to behold, the new body that was growing inside of it, and would come out of it when she died, would be ugly, and crooked this way and that, like an aged hawthorn that has lived hundreds of years exposed upon all sides to salt sea-winds.

As time went on, this disease of self-conceit went

41

on too, gradually devouring the good that was in her. For there is no fault that does not bring its brothers and sisters and cousins to live with it. By degrees, from thinking herself so clever, she came to fancy that whatever seemed to her, must of course be the correct judgment, and whatever she wished, the right thing; and grew so obstinate, that at length her parents feared to thwart her in any thing, knowing well that she would never give in. But there are victories far worse than defeats; and to overcome an angel too gentle to put out all his strength, and ride away in triumph on the back of a devil, is one of the poorest.

So long as she was left to take her own way and do as she would, she gave her parents little trouble. She would play about by herself in the little garden with its few hardy flowers, or amongst the heather where the bees were busy; or she would wander away amongst the hills, and be nobody knew where, sometimes from morning to night; nor did her parents venture to find fault with her.

She never went into rages like the princess, and would have thought Rosamond—oh, so ugly and vile! if she had seen her in one of her passions. But she was no better, for all that, and was quite as ugly in the eyes of the wise woman, who could not only see but read her face. What is there to choose between a face distorted to hideousness by anger, and one distorted to silliness by self-complacency? True, there is more hope of helping the angry child out of her form of selfishness than the conceited child out of hers; but on the other hand, the conceited child was not so terrible or dangerous as the wrathful one. The conceited one, however, was sometimes very angry, and then her anger was more spiteful than the other's; and, again, the wrathful one was often very conceited too. So that, on the whole, of two very unpleasant creatures, I would say that the king's daughter would have been the worse, had not the shepherd's been quite as bad.

But, as I have said, the wise woman had her eye upon her: she saw that something special must be done, else she would be one of those who kneel to their own shadows till feet grow on their knees; then go down on their hands till their hands grow into feet; then lay their faces on the ground till they grow into snouts; when at last they are a hideous sort of lizards, each of which believes himself the best, wisest, and loveliest being in the world, yea, the very centre of the universe. And so they run about forever looking for their own shadows, that they may worship them, and miserable because they cannot find them, being themselves too near the ground to have any shadows; and what becomes of them at last there is but one who knows.

The wise woman, therefore, one day walked up to the door of the shepherd's cottage, dressed like a poor woman, and asked for a drink of water. The shepherd's wife looked at her, liked her, and brought her a cup of milk. The wise woman took it, for she made it a rule to accept every kindness that was offered her.

Agnes was not by nature a greedy girl, as I have said; but self-conceit will go far to generate every other vice under the sun. Vanity, which is a form of self-conceit, has repeatedly shown itself as the deepest feeling in the heart of a horrible murderess.

That morning, at breakfast, her mother had stinted her in milk—just a little—that she might have enough to make some milk-porridge for their dinner. Agnes did not mind it at the time, but when she saw the milk now given to a beggar, as she called the wise woman—though, surely, one might ask a draught of water, and accept a draught of milk, without being a beggar in any such sense as Agnes's contemptuous

use of the word implied—a cloud came upon her forehead, and a double vertical wrinkle settled over her
nose. The wise woman saw it, for all her business
was with Agnes though she little knew it, and, rising,
went and offered the cup to the child, where she sat
with her knitting in a corner. Agnes looked at it, did
not want it, was inclined to refuse it from a beggar,
but thinking it would show her consequence to assert
her rights, took it and drank it up. For whoever is
possessed by a devil, judges with the mind of that
devil; and hence Agnes was guilty of such a mean-
ness as many who are themselves capable of something just as bad will consider incredible.

The wise woman waited till she had finished it—
then, looking into the empty cup, said:

"You might have given me back as much as you
had no claim upon!"

Agnes turned away and made no answer—far less
from shame than indignation.

The wise woman looked at the mother.

"You should not have offered it to her if you did
not mean her to have it," said the mother, siding with
the devil in her child against the wise woman and her
child too. Some foolish people think they take another's part when they take the part he takes.

The wise woman said nothing, but fixed her eyes
upon her, and soon the mother hid her face in her
apron weeping. Then she turned again to Agnes, who
had never looked round but sat with her back to both,
and suddenly lapped her in the folds of her cloak.
When the mother again lifted her eyes, she had
vanished.

Never supposing she had carried away her child,
but uncomfortable because of what she had said to
the poor woman, the mother went to the door, and
called after her as she toiled slowly up the hill. But

she never turned her head; and the mother went back into her cottage.

The wise woman walked close past the shepherd and his dogs, and through the midst of his block of sheep. The shepherd wondered where she could be going—right up the hill. There was something strange about her too, he thought; and he followed her with his eyes as she went up and up.

It was near sunset, and as the sun went down, a gray cloud settled on the top of the mountain, which his last rays turned into a rosy gold. Straight into this cloud the shepherd saw the woman hold her pace, and in it she vanished. He little imagined that his child was under her cloak.

He went home as usual in the evening, but Agnes had not come in. They were accustomed to such an absence now and then, and were not at first frightened; but when it grew dark and she did not appear, the husband set out with his dogs in one direction, and the wife in another, to seek their child. Morning came and they had not found her. Then the whole country-side arose to search for the missing Agnes; but day after day and night after night passed, and nothing was discovered of or concerning her, until at length all gave up the search in despair except the mother, although she was nearly convinced now that the poor woman had carried her off.

One day she had wandered some distance from her cottage, thinking she might come upon the remains of her daughter at the foot of some cliff, when she came suddenly, instead, upon a disconsolate-looking creature sitting on a stone by the side of a stream. Her hair hung in tangles from her head; her clothes were tattered, and through the rents her skin showed in many places; her cheeks were white, and worn thin with hunger; the hollows were dark under her eyes, and they stood out scared and wild. When she caught sight of the shepherdess, she jumped to her feet, and would have run away, but fell down in a faint.

At first sight the mother had taken her for her own child, but now she saw, with a pang of disappointment, that she was mistaken. Full of compassion, nevertheless, she said to herself:

"If she is not my Agnes, she is as much in need of help as if she were. If I cannot be good to my own, I will be as good as I can to some other woman's; and though I should scorn to be consoled for the loss of one by the presence of another, I yet may find some gladness in rescuing one child from the death which has taken the other."

Perhaps her words were not just like these, but her thoughts were. She took up the child, and carried her home. And this is how Rosamond came to occupy the place of the little girl whom she had envied in the picture.

VII

NOTWITHSTANDING the differences between the two girls, which were, indeed, so many that most people would have said they were not in the least alike, they were the same in this, that each cared more for her own fancies and desires than for any thing else in the world. But I will tell you another difference: the princess was like several children in one—such was the variety of her moods; and in one mood she had no recollection or care about any thing whatever belonging to a previous mood—not even if it had left her but a moment before, and had been so violent as to make her ready to put her hand in the fire to get what she wanted. Plainly she was the mere puppet of her moods, and more than that, any cunning nurse who knew her well enough could call or send away those moods almost as she pleased, like a showman pulling strings behind a show. Agnes, on the contrary, seldom changed her mood, but kept that of calm assured self-satisfaction. Father nor mother had ever by wise punishment helped her to gain a victory over herself, and do what she did not like or choose; and their folly in reasoning with one unreasonable had fixed her in her conceit. She would actually nod her head to herself in complacent pride that she had stood out against them. This, however, was not so difficult as to justify even the pride of having conquered, seeing she loved them so little, and paid so little attention to the arguments and persuasions they used. Neither, when she found herself wrapped in the dark folds of the wise woman's cloak, did she behave in the least like the princess, for she was not afraid. "She'll soon set me down," she said, too self-important to suppose that any one would dare do her an injury.

Whether it be a good thing or a bad not to be afraid depends on what the fearlessness is founded upon. Some have no fear, because they have no knowledge of the danger: there is nothing fine in that. Some are too stupid to be afraid: there is nothing fine in that. Some who are not easily frightened would yet turn their backs and run, the moment they were frightened: such never had more courage than fear. But the man who will do his work in spite of his fear is a man of true courage. The fearlessness of Agnes was only ignorance: she did not know what it was to be hurt; she had never read a single story of giant, or ogress, or wolf; and her mother had never carried out one of her threats of punishment. If the wise woman had but pinched her, she would have shown herself an abject little coward, trembling with fear at every change of motion so long as she carried her.

Nothing such, however, was in the wise woman's

plan for the curing of her. On and on she carried her without a word. She knew that if she set her down she would never run after her like the princess, at least not before the evil thing was already upon her. On and on she went, never halting, never letting the light look in, or Agnes look out. She walked very fast, and got home to her cottage very soon after the princess had gone from it.

But she did not set Agnes down either in the cottage or in the great hall. She had other places, none of them alike. The place she had chosen for Agnes was a strange one—such a one as is to be found nowhere else in the wide world.

It was a great hollow sphere, made of a substance similar to that of the mirror which Rosamond had broken, but differently compounded. That substance no one could see by itself. It had neither door, nor window, nor any opening to break its perfect roundness.

The wise woman carried Agnes into a dark room, there undressed her, took from her hand her knitting-needles, and put her, naked as she was born, into the hollow sphere.

What sort of a place it was she could not tell. She could see nothing but a faint cold bluish light all about her. She could not feel that any thing supported her, and yet she did not sink. She stood for a while, perfectly calm, then sat down. Nothing bad could happen to *her*—she was so important! And, indeed, it was but this: she had cared only for Somebody, and now she was going to have only Somebody. Her own choice was going to be carried a good deal farther for her than she would have knowingly carried it for herself.

After sitting a while, she wished she had something to do, but nothing came. A little longer, and it grew wearisome. She would see whether she could

not walk out of the strange luminous dusk that surrounded her.

Walk she found she could, well enough, but walk
out she could not. On and on she went, keeping as
much in a straight line as she might, but after walking
until she was thoroughly tired, she found herself no
nearer out of her prison than before. She had, not
indeed, advanced a single step; for, in whatever direction she tried to go, the sphere turned round and
round, answering her feet accordingly. Like a squirrel
in his cage she but kept placing another spot of the
cunningly suspended sphere under her feet, and she
would have been still only at its lowest point after
walking for ages.

At length she cried aloud; but there was no answer. It grew dreary and drearier—in her, that is:
outside there was no change. Nothing was overhead,
nothing under foot, nothing on either hand, but the
same pale, faint, bluish glimmer. She wept at last,
then grew very angry, and then sullen; but nobody
heeded whether she cried or laughed. It was all the
same to the cold unmoving twilight that rounded her.
On and on went the dreary hours—or did they go at
all?—"no change, no pause, no hope";—on and on
till she *felt* she was forgotten, and then she grew
strangely still and fell asleep.

The moment she was asleep, the wise woman
came, lifted her out, and laid her in her bosom; fed
her with a wonderful milk, which she received without knowing it; nursed her all the night long, and,
just ere she woke, laid her back in the blue sphere
again.

When first she came to herself, she thought the
horrors of the preceding day had been all a dream of
the night. But they soon asserted themselves as facts
for here they were!—nothing to see but a cold blue
light, and nothing to do but see it. Oh, how slowly

the hours went by! She lost all notion of time. If she had been told that she had been there twenty years, she would have believed it—or twenty minutes—it would have been all the same: except for weariness, time was for her no more.

Another night came, and another still, during both of which the wise woman nursed and fed her. But she knew nothing of that, and the same one dreary day seemed ever brooding over her.

All at once, on the third day, she was aware that a naked child was seated beside her. But there was something about the child that made her shudder. She never looked at Agnes, but sat with her chin sunk on her chest, and her eyes staring at her own toes. She was the color of pale earth, with a pinched nose, and a mere slit in her face for a mouth.

"How ugly she is!" thought Agnes. "What business has she beside me!"

But it was so lonely that she would have been glad to play with a serpent, and put out her hand to touch her. She touched nothing. The child, also, put out her hand—but in the direction away from Agnes. And that was well, for if she had touched Agnes it would have killed her. Then Agnes said, "Who are you?" And the little girl said, "Who are you?" "I am Agnes," said Agnes; and the little girl said, "I am Agnes." Then Agnes thought she was mocking her, and said, "You are ugly"; and the little girl said, "You are ugly."

Then Agnes lost her temper, and put out her hands to seize the little girl; but lo! the little girl was gone, and she found herself tugging at her own hair. She let go; and there was the little girl again! Agnes was furious now, and flew at her to bite her. But she found her teeth in her own arm, and the little girl was gone—only to return again; and each time she came back she was tenfold uglier than before. And now Agnes hated her with her whole heart.

The moment she hated her, it flashed upon her with a sickening disgust that the child was not another, but her Self, her Somebody, and that she was now shut up with her for ever and ever—no more for one moment ever to be alone. In her agony of despair, sleep descended, and she slept.

When she woke, there was the little girl, heedless, ugly, miserable, staring at her own toes. All at once, the creature began to smile, but with such an odious, self-satisfied expression, that Agnes felt ashamed of seeing her. Then she began to pat her own cheeks, to stroke her own body, and examine her finger-ends, nodding her head with satisfaction. Agnes felt that there could not be such another hateful, ape-like creature, and at the same time was perfectly aware she was only doing outside of her what she herself had been doing, as long as she could remember, inside of her.

She turned sick at herself, and would gladly have been put out of existence, but for three days the odious companionship went on. By the third day, Agnes was not merely sick but ashamed of the life she had hitherto led, was despicable in her own eyes, and astonished that she had never seen the truth concerning herself before.

The next morning she woke in the arms of the wise woman; the horror had vanished from her sight, and two heavenly eyes were gazing upon her. She wept and clung to her, and the more she clung, the more tenderly did the great strong arms close around her.

When she had lain thus for a while, the wise woman carried her into her cottage, and washed her in the little well; then dressed her in clean garments, and gave her bread and milk. When she had eaten it, she called her to her, and said very solemnly,—

"Agnes, you must not imagine you are cured. That you are ashamed of yourself now is no sign that the cause for such shame has ceased. In new circumstances, especially after you have done well for a while, you will be in danger of thinking just as much of yourself as before. So beware of yourself. I am going from home, and leave you in charge of the house. Do just as I tell you till my return."

She then gave her the same directions she had formerly given Rosamond—with this difference, that she told her to go into the picture-hall when she pleased, showing her the entrance, against which the clock no longer stood—and went away, closing the door behind her.

VIII

AS soon as she was left alone, Agnes set to work tidying and dusting the cottage, made up the

fire, watered the bed, and cleaned the inside of the
windows: the wise woman herself always kept the
outside of them clean. When she had done, she found
her dinner—of the same sort she was used to at
home, but better—in the hole of the wall. When she
had eaten it, she went to look at the pictures.

By this time her old disposition had begun to rouse
again. She had been doing her duty, and had in consequence begun again to think herself Somebody.
However strange it may well seem, to do one's duty
will make any one conceited who only does it sometimes. Those who do it always would as soon think
of being conceited of eating their dinner as of doing
their duty. What honest boy would pride himself on
not picking pockets? A thief who was trying to reform
would. To be conceited of doing one's duty is then a
sign of how little one does it, and how little one sees
what a contemptible thing it is not to do it. Could any
but a low creature be conceited of not being contemptible? Until our duty becomes to us common as
breathing, we are poor creatures.

So Agnes began to stroke herself once more, forgetting her late self-stroking companion, and never
reflecting that she was not doing what she had then
abhorred. And in this mood she went into the pic-
ture-gallery.

The first picture she saw represented a square in
a great city, one side of which was occupied by a
splendid marble palace, with great flights of broad
steps leading up to the door. Between it and the square
was a marble-paved court, with gates of brass, at
which stood sentries in gorgeous uniforms, and to
which was affixed the following proclamation in letters of gold, large enough for Agnes to read;—

*"By the will of the king, from this time until further
notice, every stray child found in the realm shall be*

brought without a moment's delay to the palace. Whoever shall be found having done otherwise shall straightway lose his head by the hand of the public executioner."

Agnes's heart beat loud, and her face flushed.

"Can there by such a city in the world?" she said to herself. "If I only knew where it was, I should set out for it at once. *There* would be the place for a clever girl like me!"

Her eyes fell on the picture which had so enticed Rosamond. It was the very country where her father fed his flocks. Just round the shoulder of the hill was the cottage where her parents lived, where she was born and whence she had been carried by the beggar-woman.

"Ah!" she said, "they didn't know me there. They little thought what I could be, if I had the chance. If I were but in this good, kind, loving, generous king's palace, I should soon be such a great lady as they never saw! Then they would understand what a good little girl I had always been! And I shouldn't forget my poor parents like some I have read of. *I* should never be selfish and proud like girls in story-books!"

As she said this, she turned her back with disdain upon the picture of her home, and setting herself before the picture of the palace, stared at it with wide ambitious eyes, and a heart whose every beat was a throb of arrogant self-esteem.

The shepherd-child was now worse than ever the poor princess had been. For the wise woman had given her a terrible lesson, one of which the princess was not capable, and she had known what it meant; yet here she was as bad as ever, therefore worse than before. The ugly creature whose presence had made her so miserable had indeed crept out of sight and mind too—but where was she? Nestling in her very heart, where most of all she had her company and least of all could see her. The wise woman had called her out, that Agnes might see what sort of creature she was herself; but now she was snug in her soul's bed again, and she did not even suspect she was there.

After gazing a while at the palace picture, during which her ambitious pride rose and rose, she turned yet again in condescending mood, and honored the home picture with one stare more.

"What a poor, miserable spot it is compared with this lordly palace!" she said.

But presently she spied something in it she had not seen before, and drew nearer. It was the form of a little girl, building a bridge of stones over one of the hill-brooks.

"Ah, there I am myself!" she said. "That is just how I used to do.—No," she resumed, "it is not me. That snub-nosed little fright could never be meant for me! It was the frock that made me think so. But it *is* a picture of the place. I declare, I can see the smoke of the cottage rising from behind the hill! What a dull, dirty, insignificant spot it is! And what a life to lead there!"

She turned once more to the city picture. And now a strange thing took place. In proportion as the other, to the eyes of her mind, receded into the background, this, to her present bodily eyes, appeared to come forward and assume reality. At last, after it had been in this way growing upon her for some time, she gave a cry of conviction, and said aloud,—

"I do believe it is real! That frame is only a trick of the woman to make me fancy it a picture lest I should go and make my fortune. She is a witch, the ugly old creature! It would serve her right to tell the king and have her punished for not taking me to the palace— one of his poor lost children he is so fond of! I should like to see her ugly old head cut off. Anyhow I will try my luck without asking her leave. How she has ill used me!"

But at that moment, she heard the voice of the wise woman calling, "Agnes!" and, smoothing her face, she tried to look as good as she could, and walked back into the cottage. There stood the wise woman, looking all round the place, and examining her work. She fixed her eyes upon Agnes in a way that confused her, and made her cast hers down, for she felt as if she were reading her thoughts. The wise woman, however, asked no questions, but began to talk about her work, approving of some of it, which filled her with arrogance, and showing how some of it might have been done better, which filled her with resentment. But the wise woman seemed to take no care of what she might be thinking, and went straight on with her lesson. By the time it was over, the power of reading thoughts would not have been necessary to a knowledge of what was in the mind of Agnes, for it had all come to the surface—that is up into her face, which is the surface of the mind. Ere it had time to sink down again, the wise woman caught up the little mirror, and held it before her: Agnes saw her Somebody—the very embodiment of miserable conceit and ugly ill-temper. She gave such a scream of horror that the wise woman pitied her, and laying aside the mirror, took her upon her knees, and talked to her most kindly and solemnly; in particular about the necessity of destroying the ugly things that come out of the heart—so ugly that they make the very face over them ugly also.

And what was Agnes doing all the time the wise woman was talking to her? Would you believe it?—instead of thinking how to kill the ugly things in her heart, she was with all her might resolving to be more careful of her face, that is, to keep down the things

56

in her heart so that they should not show in her face, she was resolving to be a hypocrite as well as a self-worshipper. Her heart was wormy, and the worms were eating very fast at it now.

Then the wise woman laid her gently down upon the heather-bed, and she fell asleep, and had an awful dream about her Somebody.

When she woke in the morning, instead of getting up to do the work of the house, she lay thinking—to evil purpose. In place of taking her dream as a warning, and thinking over what the wise woman had said the night before, she communed with herself in this fashion:—

"If I stay here longer, I shall be miserable. It is nothing better than slavery. The old witch shows me horrible things in the day to set me dreaming horrible things in the night. If I don't run away, that frightful blue prison and the disgusting girl will come back, and I shall go out of my mind. How I do wish I could find the way to the good king's palace! I shall go and look at the picture again—if it be a picture—as soon as I've got my clothes on. The work can wait. It's not my work. It's the old witch's; and she ought to do it herself."

She jumped out of bed, and hurried on her clothes. There was no wise woman to be seen; and she hastened into the hall. There was the picture, with the marble palace, and the proclamation shining in letters of gold upon its gates of brass. She stood before it, and gazed and gazed; and all the time it kept growing upon her in some strange way, until at last she was fully persuaded that it was no picture, but a real city, square, and marble palace, seen through a framed opening in the wall. She ran up to the frame, stepped over it, felt the wind blow upon her check, heard the sound of a closing door behind her, and was free. *Free* was she, with that creature inside her?

The same moment a terrible storm of thunder and lightning, wind and rain, came on. The uproar was appalling. Agnes threw herself upon the ground, hid her face in her hands, and there lay until it was over. As soon as she felt the sun shining on her, she rose. There was the city far away on the horizon. Without once turning to take a farewell look of the place she was leaving, she set off, as fast as her feet would carry her, in the direction of the city. So eager was she, that again and again she fell, but only to get up, and run on faster than before.

IX

THE shepherdess carried Rosamond home, gave her a warm bath in the tub in which she washed her linen, made her some bread and milk, and after she had eaten it, put her to bed in Agnes's crib, where she slept all the rest of that day and all the following night.

When at last she opened her eyes, it was to see around her a far poorer cottage than the one she had left—very bare and uncomfortable indeed, she might well have thought; but she had come through such troubles of late, in the way of hunger and weariness and cold and fear, that she was not altogether in her ordinary mood of fault-finding, and so was able to lie enjoying the thought that at length she was safe, and going to be fed and kept warm. The idea of doing any thing in return for shelter and food and clothes, did not, however, even cross her mind.

But the shepherdess was one of that plentiful number who can be wiser concerning other women's children than concerning their own. Such will often give you very tolerable hints as to how you ought to manage your children, and will find fault neatly enough with the system you are trying to carry out; but all their wisdom goes off in talking, and there is none left for doing what they have themselves said. There is one road talk never finds, and that is the way into the talker's own hands and feet. And such never seem to know themselves—not even when they are reading about themselves in print. Still, not being specially blinded in any direction but their own, they can sometimes even act with a little sense towards children who are not theirs. They are affected with a sort of blindness like that which renders some people incapable of seeing, except sideways.

She came up to the bed, looked at the princess, and saw that she was better. But she did not like her much. There was no mark of a princess about her, and never had been since she began to run alone. True, hunger had brought down her fat cheeks, but it had not turned down her impudent nose, or driven the sullenness and greed from her mouth. Nothing but the wise woman could do that—and not even she, without the aid of the princess herself. So the shepherdess thought what a poor substitute she had got for her own lovely Agnes—who was in fact equally repulsive, only in a way to which she had got used; for the selfishness in her love had blinded her to the thin pinched nose and the mean self-satisfied mouth. It was well for the princess, though, sad as it is to say, that the shepherdess did not take to her, for then she would most likely have only done her harm instead of good.

"Now, my girl," she said, "you must get up, and do something. We can't keep idle folk here."

"I'm not a folk," said Rosamond; "I'm a princess."

"A pretty princess—with a nose like that! And all in rags too! If you tell such stories, I shall soon let you know what I think of you."

Rosamond then understood that the mere calling herself a princess, without having any thing to show for it, was of no use. She obeyed and rose, for she was hungry; but she had to sweep the floor ere she had any thing to eat.

The shepherd came in to breakfast, and was kinder than his wife. He took her up in his arms and would have kissed her; but she took it as an insult from a man whose hands smelt of tar, and kicked and screamed with rage. The poor man, finding he had made a mistake, set her down at once. But to look at the two, one might well have judged it condescension rather than rudeness in such a man to kiss such a child. He was tall, and almost stately, with a thoughtful forehead, bright eyes, eagle nose, and gentle mouth; while the princess was such as I have described her.

Not content with being set down and let alone, she continued to storm and scold at the shepherd, crying she was a princess, and would like to know what right he had to touch her! But he only looked down upon her from the height of his tall person with a benignant smile, regarding her as a spoiled little ape whose mother had flattered her by calling her a princess.

"Turn her out of doors, the ungrateful hussy!" cried his wife. "With your bread and your milk inside her ugly body, this is what she gives you for it! Troth, I'm paid for carrying home such an ill-bred tramp in my arms! My own poor angel Agnes! As if that ill-tempered toad were one hair like her!"

These words drove the princess beside herself; for those who are most given to abuse can least endure it. With fists and feet and teeth, as was her wont, she rushed at the shepherdess, whose hand was already raised to deal her a sound box on the ear, when a better appointed minister of vengeance suddenly showed himself. Bounding in at the cottage-door came one of the sheep-dogs, who was called Prince, and whom I shall not refer to with a *which*, because he was a very superior animal indeed, even for a sheep-dog, which is the most intelligent of dogs: he flew at the princess, knocked her down, and commenced shaking her so violently as to tear her miserable clothes to pieces. Used, however, to mouthing little lambs, he took care not to hurt her much, though for her good he left her a blue nip or two by way of letting her imagine what biting might be. His master, know-ing he would not injure her, thought it better not to call him off, and in half a minute he left her of his own accord, and, casting a glance of indignant rebuke behind him as he went, walked slowly to the hearth, where he laid himself down with his tail toward her. She rose, terrified almost to death, and would have crept again into Agnes's crib for refuge; but the shep-herdess cried—

"Come, come, princess! I'll have no skulking to bed in the good daylight. Go and clean your master's Sunday boots there."

"I will not!" screamed the princess, and ran from the house.

"Prince!" cried the shepherdess, and up jumped the dog, and looked in her face, wagging his bushy tail.

"Fetch her back," she said, pointing to the door.

With two or three bounds Prince caught the prin-cess, again threw her down, and taking her by her clothes dragged her back into the cottage, and dropped her at his mistress' feet, where she lay like a bundle of rags.

"Get up," said the shepherdess.

Rosamond got up as pale as death.

"Go and clean the boots."

"I don't know how."

"Go and try. There are the brushes, and yonder is the blacking-pot."

Instructing her how to black boots, it came into

the thought of the shepherdess what a fine thing it would be if she could teach this miserable little wretch, so forsaken and ill-bred, to be a good, well-behaved, respectable child. She was hardly the woman to do it, but every thing well meant is a help, and she had the wisdom to beg her husband to place Prince under her orders for a while, and not take him to the hill as usual, that he might help her in getting the princess into order.

When the husband was gone, and his boots, with the aid of her own finishing touches, at last quite respectably brushed, the shepherdess told the princess that she might go and play for a while, only she must not go out of sight of the cottage-door.

The princess went right gladly, with the firm intention, however, of getting out of sight by slow degrees, and then at once taking to her heels. But no sooner was she over the threshold than the shepherdess said to the dog, "Watch her;" and out shot Prince.

The moment she saw him, Rosamond threw herself on her face, trembling from head to foot. But the dog had no quarrel with her, and of the violence against which he always felt bound to protest in dog fashion, there was no sign in the prostrate shape before him; so he poked his nose under her, turned her over, and began licking her face and hands. When she saw that he meant to be friendly, her love for animals, which had had no indulgence for a long time now, came wide awake, and in a little while they were romping and rushing about, the best friends in the world.

Having thus seen one enemy, as she thought, changed to a friend, she began to resume her former plan, and crept cunningly farther and farther. At length she came to a little hollow, and instantly rolled down into it. Finding then that she was out of sight of the cottage, she ran off at full speed.

But she had not gone more than a dozen paces, when she heard a growling rush behind her, and the next instant was on the ground, with the dog standing over her, showing his teeth, and flaming at her with his eyes. She threw her arms round his neck, and immediately he licked her face, and let her get up. But the moment she would have moved a step farther from the cottage, there he was in front of her, growling, and showing his teeth. She saw it was of no use, and went back with him.

Thus was the princess provided with a dog for a private tutor—just the right sort for her.

Presently the shepherdess appeared at the door and called her. She would have disregarded the summons, but Prince did his best to let her know that, until she could obey herself, she must obey him. So she went into the cottage, and there the shepherdess ordered her to peel the potatoes for dinner. She sulked and refused. Here Prince could do nothing to help his mistress, but she had not to go far to find another ally.

"Very well, Miss Princess!" she said, "we shall soon see how you like to go without when dinner-time comes."

Now the princess had very little foresight, and the idea of future hunger would have moved her little; but happily, from her game of romps with Prince, she had begun to be hungry already, and so the threat had force. She took the knife and began to peel the potatoes.

By slow degrees the princess improved a little. A few more outbreaks of passion, and a few more savage attacks from Prince, and she had learned to try to restrain herself when she felt the passion coming on; while a few dinnerless afternoons entirely opened her eyes to the necessity of working in order to eat.

Prince was her first, and Hunger her second dog-counsellor.

But a still better thing was that she soon grew very fond of Prince. Towards the gaining of her affections, he had three advantages: first, his nature was inferior to hers; next, he was a beast; and last, she was afraid of him; for so spoiled was she that she could more easily love what was below than what was above her, and a beast, than one of her own kind, and indeed could hardly have ever come to love any thing much that she had not first learned to fear, and the white teeth and flaming eyes of the angry Prince were more terrible to her than any thing had yet been, except those of the wolf, which she had now forgotten. Then again, he was such a delightful playfellow, that so long as she neither lost her temper, nor went against orders, she might do almost any thing she pleased with him. In fact, such was his influence upon her, that she who had scoffed at the wisest woman in the whole world, and derided the wishes of her own father and mother, came at length to regard this dog as a superior being, and to look up to him as well as love him. And this was best of all.

The improvement upon her, in the course of a month, was plain. She had quite ceased to go into passions, and had actually begun to take a little interest in her work and try to do it well.

Still, the change was mostly an outside one. I do not mean that she was pretending. Indeed she had never been given to pretence of any sort. But the change was not in *her*, only in her mood. A second change of circumstances would have soon brought a second change of behavior; and, so long as that was possible, she continued the same sort of person she had always been. But if she had not gained much, a trifle had been gained for her: a little quietness and order of mind, and hence a somewhat greater possibility of the first idea of right arising in it, whereupon she would begin to see what a wretched creature she was, and must continue until she herself was right.

Meantime the wise woman had been watching her when she least fancied it, and taking note of the change that was passing upon her. Out of the large eyes of a gentle sheep she had been watching her—a sheep that puzzled the shepherd; for every now and then she would appear in his flock, and he would catch sight of her two or three times in a day, sometimes for days together, yet he never saw her when he looked for her, and never when he counted the flock into the fold at night. He knew she was not one of his; but where could she come from, and where could she go to? For there was no other flock within many miles, and he never could get near enough to her to see whether or not she was marked. Nor was Prince of the least use to him for the unravelling of the mystery; for although, as often as he told him to fetch the strange sheep, he went bounding to her at once, it was only to lie down at her feet.

At length, however, the wise woman had made up her mind, and after that the strange sheep no longer troubled the shepherd.

As Rosamond improved, the shepherdess grew kinder. She gave her all Agnes's clothes, and began to treat her much more like a daughter. Hence she had a great deal of liberty after the little work required of her was over, and would often spend hours at a time with the shepherd, watching the sheep and the dogs, and learning a little from seeing how Prince, and the others as well, managed their charge—how they never touched the sheep that did as they were told and turned when they were bid, but jumped on a disobedient flock, and ran along their backs, biting, and barking, and half choking themselves with mouthfuls of their wool.

Then also she would play with the brooks and learn their songs, and build bridges over them. And sometimes she would be seized with such delight of heart that she would spread out her arms to the wind, and go rushing up the hill till her breath left her, when she would tumble down in the heather, and lie there till it came back again.

A noticeable change had by this time passed also on her countenance. Her coarse shapeless mouth had begun to show a glimmer of lines and curves about it, and the fat had not returned with the roses to her cheeks, so that her eyes looked larger than before; while, more noteworthy still, the bridge of her nose had grown higher, so that it was less of the impudent, insignificant thing inherited from a certain great-great-great-grandmother, who had little else to leave her. For a long time, it had fitted her very well, for it was just like her; but now there was ground for alteration, and already the granny who gave it her would not have recognized it. It was growing a little like Prince's; and Prince's was a long, perceptive, sagacious nose,—one that was seldom mistaken.

One day about noon, while the sheep were mostly lying down, and the shepherd, having left them to the care of the dogs, was himself stretched under the shade of a rock a little way apart, and the princess sat knitting, with Prince at her feet, lying in wait for a snap at a great fly, for even he had his follies— Rosamond saw a poor woman come toiling up the hill, but took little notice of her until she was passing, a few yards off, when she heard her utter the dog's name in a low voice.

Immediately on the summons, Prince started up and followed her—with hanging head, but gently-wagging tail. At first the princess thought he was merely taking observations, and consulting with his nose whether she was respectable or not, but she soon saw that he was following her in meek submission. Then she sprung to her feet and cried, "Prince, Prince!" But Prince only turned his head and gave her an odd look, as if he were trying to smile, and could not. Then the princess grew angry, and ran after him, shouting, "Prince, come here directly." Again Prince turned his head, but this time to growl and show his teeth.

The princess flew into one of her forgotten rages, and picking up a stone, flung it at the woman. Prince turned and darted at her, with fury in his eyes, and his white teeth gleaming. At the awful sight the princess turned also, and would have fled, but he was upon her in a moment, and threw her to the ground, and there she lay.

It was evening when she came to herself. A cool twilight wind, that somehow seemed to come all the way from the stars, was blowing upon her. The poor woman and Prince, the shepherd and his sheep, were all gone, and she was left alone with the wind upon the heather.

She felt sad, weak, and, perhaps, for the first time in her life, a little ashamed. The violence of which she had been guilty had vanished from her spirit, and now lay in her memory with the calm morning behind it, while in front the quiet dusky night was now closing in the loud shame betwixt a double peace. Between the two her passion looked ugly. It pained her to remember. She felt it was hateful, and *hers*.

But, alas, Prince was gone! That horrid woman had taken him away! The fury rose again in her heart, and raged—until it came to her mind how her dear Prince would have flown at her throat if he had seen her in such a passion. The memory calmed her, and she rose and went home. There, perhaps, she would find Prince, for surely he could never have been such a silly dog as go away altogether with a strange woman!

She opened the door and went in. Dogs were asleep all about the cottage, it seemed to her, but nowhere was Prince. She crept away to her little bed, and cried herself asleep.

In the morning the shepherd and shepherdess were indeed glad to find she had come home, for they thought she had run away.

"Where is Prince?" she cried, the moment she waked.

"His mistress has taken him," answered the shepherd.

"Was that woman his mistress?"

"I fancy so. He followed her as if he had known her all his life. I am very sorry to lose him, though."

The poor woman had gone close past the rock where the shepherd lay. He saw her coming, and thought of the strange sheep which had been feeding beside him when he lay down. "Who can she be?" he said to himself; but when he noted how Prince followed her, without even looking up at him as he passed, he remembered how Prince had come to him. And this was how: as he lay in bed one fierce winter morning, just about to rise, he heard the voice of a woman call to him through the storm, "Shepherd, I have brought you a dog. Be good to him. I will come again and fetch him away." He dressed as quickly as he could, and went to the door. It was half snowed up, but on the top of the white mound before it stood Prince. And now he had gone as mysteriously as he had come, and he felt sad.

Rosamond was very sorry too, and hence when she saw the looks of the shepherd and shepherdess, she was able to understand them. And she tried for a while to behave better to them because of their sorrow. So the loss of the dog brought them all nearer to each other.

X

AFTER the thunder-storm, Agnes did not meet with a single obstruction or misadventure. Everybody was strangely polite, gave her whatever she desired, and answered her questions, but asked none in return, and looked all the time as if her departure would be a relief. They were afraid, in fact, from her appearance, lest she should tell them that she was lost, when they would be bound, on pain of public execution, to take her to the palace.

But no sooner had she entered the city than she saw it would hardly do to present herself as a lost child at the palace-gates; for how were they to know that she was not an imposter, especially since she really was one, having run away from the wise woman? So she wandered about looking at every thing until she was tired, and bewildered by the noise and confusion all around her. The wearier she got, the more was she pushed in every direction. Having been used to a whole hill to wander upon, she was very awkward in the crowded streets, and often on the point of being run over by the horses, which seemed to her to be going every way like a frightened flock. She spoke to several persons, but no one stopped to answer her; and at length, her courage giving way, she felt lost indeed, and began to cry. A soldier saw her, and asked what was the matter.

"I've nowhere to go to," she sobbed.

"Where's your mother?" asked the soldier.

"I don't know," answered Agnes. "I was carried off by an old woman, who then went away and left me. I don't know where she is, or where I am myself."

"Come," said the soldier, "this is a case for his majesty."

So saying, he took her by the hand, led her to the

69

palace, and begged an audience of the king and queen. The porter glanced at Agnes, immediately admitted them, and showed them into a great splendid room, where the king and queen sat every day to review lost children, in the hope of one day thus finding their Rosamond. But they were by this time beginning to get tired of it. The moment they cast their eyes upon Agnes, the queen threw back her head, threw up her hands, and cried, "What a miserable, conceited, white-faced ape!" and the king turned upon the soldier in wrath, and cried, forgetting his own decree, "What do you mean by bringing such a dirty, vulgar-looking, pert creature into my palace? The dullest soldier in my army could never for a moment imagine a child like *that*, one hair's-breadth like the lovely angel we lost!"

"I humbly beg your majesty's pardon," said the soldier, "but what was I to do? There stands your majesty's proclamation in gold letters on the brazen gates of the palace."

"I shall have it taken down," said the king. "Remove the child."

"Please, your majesty, what am I to do with her?"

"Take her home with you."

"I have six already, sire, and do not want her."

"Then drop her where you picked her up."

"If I do, sire, some one else will find her and bring her back to your majesties."

"That will never do," said the king. "I cannot bear to look at her."

"For all her ugliness," said the queen, "she is plainly lost, and so is our Rosamond."

"It may be only a pretence, to get into the palace," said the king.

"Take her to the head scullion, soldier," said the queen, "and tell her to make her useful. If she should find out she has been pretending to be lost, she must let me know."

The soldier was so anxious to get rid of her, that he caught her up in his arms, hurried her from the room, found his way to the scullery, and gave her, trembling with fear, in charge to the head maid, with the queen's message.

As it was evident that the queen had no favor for her, the servants did as they pleased with her, and often treated her harshly. Not one amongst them liked her, nor was it any wonder, seeing that, with every step she took from the wise woman's house, she had grown more contemptible, for she had grown more conceited. Every civil answer given her, she attributed to the impression she made, not to the desire to get rid of her; and every kindness, to approbation of her looks and speech, instead of friendliness to a lonely child. Hence by this time she was twice as odious as before; for whoever has had such severe treatment as the wise woman gave her, and is not the better for it, always grows worse than before. They drove her about, boxed her ears on the smallest provocation, laid every thing to her charge, called her all manner of contemptuous names, jeered and scoffed at her awkwardnesses, and made her life so miserable that she was in a fair way to forget every thing she had learned, and know nothing but how to clean saucepans and kettles.

They would not have been so hard upon her, however, but for her irritating behavior. She dared not refuse to do as she was told, but she obeyed now with a pursed-up mouth, and now with a contemptuous smile. The only think that sustained her was her constant contriving how to get out of the painful position in which she found herself. There is but one true way, however, of getting out of any position we may be in, and that is, to do the work of it so well that we grow fit for a better: I need not say this was not the plan upon which Agnes was cunning enough to fix.

She had soon learned from the talk around her the reason of the proclamation which had brought her hither.

"Was the lost princess so very beautiful?" she said one day to the youngest of her fellow-servants.

"Beautiful!" screamed the maid; "she was just the ugliest little toad you ever set eyes upon."

"What was she like?" asked Agnes.

"She was about your size, and quite as ugly, only not in the same way; for she had red cheeks, and a cocked little nose, and the biggest, ugliest mouth you ever saw."

Agnes fell a-thinking.

"Is there a picture of her anywhere in the palace?" she asked.

"How should I know? You can ask a housemaid."

Agnes soon learned that there was one, and contrived to get a peep of it. Then she was certain of what she had suspected from the description of her, namely, that she was the same she had seen in the picture at the wise woman's house. The conclusion followed, that the lost princess must be staying with her father and mother, for assuredly in the picture she wore one of her frocks.

She went to the head scullion, and with a humble manner, but proud heart, begged her to procure for her the favor of a word with the queen.

"A likely thing indeed!" was the answer, accompanied by a resounding box on the ear.

She tried the head cook next, but with no better success, and so was driven to her meditations again, the result of which was that she began to drop hints that she knew something about the princess. This came at length to the queen's ears, and she sent for her.

Absorbed in her own selfish ambitions, Agnes never thought of the risk to which she was about to expose her parents, but told the queen that in her wanderings she had caught sight of just such a lovely creature as she described the princess, only dressed like a peasant—saying, that, if the king would permit her to go and look for her, she had little doubt of bringing her back safe and sound within a few weeks.

But although she spoke the truth, she had such a look of cunning on her pinched face, that the queen could not possibly trust her, but believed that she made the proposal merely to get away, and have money given her for her journey. Still there was a chance, and she would not say any thing until she had consulted the king.

Then they had Agnes up before the lord chancellor, who, after much questioning of her, arrived at last, he thought, at some notion of the part of the country described by her—that was, if she spoke the truth, which, from her looks and behavior, he also considered entirely doubtful. Thereupon she was ordered back to the kitchen, and a band of soldiers, under a clever lawyer, sent out to search every foot of the supposed region. They were commanded not to return until they brought with them, bound hand and foot, such a shepherd pair as that of which they received a full description.

And now Agnes was worse off than before. For to her other miseries was added the fear of what would befall her when it was discovered that the persons of whom they were in quest, and whom she was certain they must find, were her own father and mother.

By this time the king and queen were so tired of seeing lost children, genuine or pretended—for they cared for no child any longer than there seemed a chance of its turning out their child—that with this new hope, which, however poor and vague at first, soon began to grow upon such imaginations as they had, they commanded the proclamation to be taken down from the palace gates, and directed the various sentries to admit no child whatever, lost or found, be the reason or pretence what it might, until further orders.

"I'm sick of children!" said the king to his secretary, as he finished dictating the direction.

XI

AFTER Prince was gone, the princess, by degrees, fell back into some of her bad old ways, from which only the presence of the dog, not her own betterment, had kept her. She never grew nearly so selfish again, but she began to let her angry old self lift up its head once more, until by and by she grew so bad that the shepherdess declared she should not stop in the house a day longer, for she was quite unendurable.

"It is all very well for you, husband," she said, "for you haven't her all day about you, and only see the best of her. But if you have her in work instead of play hours, you would like her no better than I do. And then it's not her ugly passions only, but when she's in one of her tantrums, it's impossible to get any work out of her. At such times she's just as obstinate as—as—as"—

She was going to say "as Agnes," but the feelings of a mother overcame her, and she could not utter the words.

"In fact," she said instead, "she makes my life miserable."

The shepherd felt he had no right to tell his wife she must submit to have her life made miserable, and therefore, although he was really much attached to Rosamond, he would not interfere; and the shepherdess told her she must look out for another place.

The princess was, however, this much better than

before, even in respect of her passions, that they were not quite so bad, and after one was over, she was really ashamed of it. But not once, ever since the departure of Prince, had she tried to check the rush of the evil temper when it came upon her. She hated it when she was out of it, and that was something; but while she was in it, she went full swing with it wherever the prince of the power of it pleased to carry her. Nor was this all: although she might by this time have known well enough that as soon as she was out of it she was certain to be ashamed of it, she would yet justify it to herself with twenty different arguments that looked very poor indeed afterwards, if then she had even remembered them.

She was not sorry to leave the shepherd's cottage, for she felt certain of soon finding her way back to her father and mother; and she would, indeed, have set out long before, but that her foot had somehow got hurt when Prince gave her his last admonition, and she had never since been able for long walks, which she sometimes blamed as the cause of her temper growing worse. But if people are good-tempered only when they are comfortable, what thanks have they?—Her foot was now much better; and as soon as the shepherdess had thus spoken, she resolved to set out at once, and work or beg her way home. At the moment she was quite unmindful of what she owed the good people, and, indeed, was as yet incapable of understanding a tenth part of her obligation to them. So she bade them good-bye without a tear, and limped her way down the hill, leaving the shepherdess weeping, and the shepherd looking very grave.

When she reached the valley she followed the course of the stream, knowing only that it would lead her away from the hill where the sheep fed, into richer lands where were farms and cattle. Rounding one of the roots of the hill she saw before her a poor woman walking slowly along the road with a burden of heather upon her back, and presently passed her, but had gone only a few paces farther when she heard her calling after her in a kind old voice—

"Your shoe-tie is loose, my child."

But Rosamond was growing tired, for her foot had become painful, and so she was cross, and neither returned answer, nor paid heed to the warning. For when we are cross, all our other faults grow busy, and poke up their ugly heads like maggots, and the princess's old dislike to doing any thing that came to her with the least air of advice about it returned in full force.

"My child," said the woman again, "if you don't fasten your shoe-tie, it will make you fall."

"Mind your own business," said Rosamond, without even turning her head, and had not gone more than three steps when she fell flat on her face on the path. She tried to get up, but the effort forced from her a scream, for she had sprained the ankle of the foot that was already lame.

The old woman was by her side instantly.

"Where are your hurt, child?" she asked, throwing down her burden and kneeling beside her.

"Go away," screamed Rosamond. "*You* made me fall, you bad woman!"

The woman made no reply, but began to feel her joints, and soon discovered the sprain. Then, in spite of Rosamond's abuse, and the violent pushes and even kicks she gave her, she took the hurt ankle in her hands, and stroked and pressed it, gently kneading it, as it were, with her thumbs, as if coaxing every particle of muscles into its right place. Nor had she done so long before Rosamond lay still. At length she ceased, and said:—

"Now, my child, you may get up."

"I can't get up, and I'm not your child," cried Rosamond. "Go away."

Without another word the woman left her, took up her burden, and continued her journey.

In a little while Rosamond tried to get up, and not only succeeded, but found she could walk, and, indeed, presently discovered that her ankle and foot also were now perfectly well.

"I wasn't much hurt after all," she said to herself, nor sent a single grateful thought after the poor woman, whom she speedily passed once more upon the road without even a greeting.

Late in the afternoon she came to a spot where the path divided into two, and was taking the one she liked the looks of better, when she started at the sound of the poor woman's voice, whom she thought she had left far behind, again calling her. She looked round, and there she was, toiling under her load of heather as before.

"You are taking the wrong turn, child," she cried.

"How can you tell that?" said Rosamond. "You know nothing about where I want to go."

"I know that road will take you where you don't want to go," said the woman.

"I shall know when I get there, then," returned Rosamond, "and no thanks to you."

She set off running. The woman took the other path, and was soon out of sight.

By and by, Rosamond found herself in the midst of a peat-moss—a flat, lonely, dismal, black country. She thought, however, that the road would soon lead her across to the other side of it among the farms, and went on without anxiety. But the stream, which had hitherto been her guide, had now vanished; and when it began to grow dark, Rosamond found that she could no longer distinguish the track. She turned, therefore, but only to find that the same darkness covered it behind as well as before. Still she made the attempt to go back by keeping as direct a line as she could, for the path was straight as an arrow. But she could not see enough even to start her in a line, and she had not gone far before she found herself hemmed in, apparently on every side, by ditches and pools of black, dismal, slimy water. And now it was so dark that she could see nothing more than the gleam of a bit of clear sky now and then in the water. Again and again she stepped knee-deep in black mud, and once tumbled down in the shallow edge of a terrible pool; after which she gave up the attempt to escape the meshes of the watery net, stood still, and began to cry bitterly, despairingly. She saw now that her un-reasonable anger had made her foolish as well as rude, and felt that she was justly punished for her wickedness to the poor woman who had been so friendly to her. What would Prince think of her, if he knew? She cast herself on the ground, hungry, and cold, and weary.

Presently, she thought she saw long creatures come heaving out of the black pools. A toad jumped upon her, and she shrieked, and sprang to her feet, and would have run away headlong, when she spied in the distance a faint glimmer. She thought it was a Will-o'-the-wisp. What could he be after? Was he look-ing for her? She dared not run, lest he should see and pounce upon her. The light came nearer, and grew brighter and larger. Plainly, the little fiend was look-ing for her—he would torment her. After many twist-ings and turnings among the pools, it came straight towards her, and she would have shrieked, but that terror made her dumb.

It came nearer and nearer, and lo! it was borne by a dark figure, with a burden on its back: it was the poor woman, and no demon, that was looking for her! She gave a scream of joy, fell down weeping at her feet, and clasped her knees. Then the poor woman threw away her burden, laid down her lantern, took the princess up in her arms, folded her cloak around her, and having taken up her lantern again, carried her slowly and carefully through the midst of the black pools, winding hither and thither. All night long she carried her thus, slowly and wearily, until at length the darkness grew a little thinner, an uncertain hint of light came from the east, and the poor woman, stopping on the brow of a little hill, opened her cloak, and set the princess down.

"I can carry you no farther," she said. "Sit there on the grass till the light comes. I will stand here by you."

Rosamond had been asleep. Now she rubbed her eyes and looked, but it was too dark to see any thing more than that there was a sky over her head. Slowly the light grew, until she could see the form of the poor woman standing in front of her; and as it went on growing, she began to think she had seen her somewhere before, till all at once she thought of the wise woman, and saw it must be she. Then she was so ashamed that she bent down her head, and could look at her no longer. But the poor woman spoke, and the voice was that of the wise woman, and every word went deep into the heart of the princess.

"Rosamond," she said, "all this time, ever since I carried you from your father's palace, I have been doing what I could to make you a lovely creature: ask yourself how far I have succeeded."

All her past story, since she found herself first under the wise woman's cloak, arose, and glided past the inner eyes of the princess, and she saw, and in a measure understood, it all. But she sat with her eyes on the ground, and made no sign.

Then said the wise woman:—

"Below there is the forest which surrounds my

house. I am going home. If you please to come there to me, I will help you, in a way I could not do now, to be good and lovely. I will wait you there all day, but if you start at once, you may be there long before noon. I shall have your breakfast waiting for you. One thing more: the beasts have not yet all gone home to their holes; but I give you my word, not one will touch you so long as you keep coming nearer to my house."

She ceased. Rosamond sat waiting to hear something more; but nothing came. She looked up; she was alone.

Alone once more! Always being left alone, because she would not yield to what was right! Oh, how safe she had felt under the wise woman's cloak! She had indeed been good to her, and she had in return behaved like one of the hyenas of the awful wood! What a wonderful house it was she lived in! And again all her own story came up into her brain from her repentant heart.

"Why didn't she take me with her?" she said. "I would have gone gladly." And she wept. But her own conscience told her that, in the very middle of her shame and desire to be good, she had returned no answer to the words of the wise woman; she had sat like a tree-stump, and done nothing. She tried to say there was nothing to be done; but she knew at once that she could have told the wise woman she had been very wicked, and asked her to take her with her. Now there was nothing to be done.

"Nothing to be done!" said her conscience. "Cannot you rise, and walk down the hill, and through the wood?"

"But the wild beasts!"

"There it is! You don't believe the wise woman yet! Did she not tell you the beasts would not touch you?"

"But they are so horrid!"

"Yes, they are; but it would be far better to be eaten up alive by them than live on—such a worthless creature as you are. Why, you're not fit to be thought about by any but bad, ugly creatures."

This was how her Self talked to her.

XII

ALL at once she jumped to her feet, and ran at full speed down the hill and into the wood. She heard howlings and yellings on all sides of her, but she ran straight on, as near as she could judge. Her spirits rose as she ran. Suddenly she saw before her, in the dusk of the thick wood, a group of some dozen wolves and hyenas, standing all together right in her way, with their green eyes fixed upon her staring. She faltered one step, then bethought her of what the wise woman had promised, and keeping straight on, dashed right into the middle of them. They fled howling, as if she had struck them with fire. She was no more afraid after that, and ere the sun was up she was out of the wood and upon the heath, which no bad thing could step upon and live. With the first peep of the sun above the horizon, she saw the little cottage before her, and ran as fast as she could run towards it. When she came near it, she saw that the door was open, and ran straight into the outstretched arms of the wise woman.

The wise woman kissed her and stroked her hair, set her down by the fire, and gave her a bowl of bread and milk.

When she had eaten it she drew her before her where she sat, and spoke to her thus:—

"Rosamond, if you would be a blessed creature instead of a mere wretch, you must submit to be tried."

"Is that something terrible?" asked the princess, turning white.

"No, my child; but it is something very difficult to come well out of. Nobody who has not been tried knows how difficult it is; but whoever has come well out of it, and those who do not overcome never do come out of it, always looks back with horror, not on what she has come through, but on the very idea of the possibility of having failed, and being still the same miserable creature as before."

"You will tell me what it is before it begins?" said the princess.

"I will not tell you exactly. But I will tell you some things to help you. One great danger is that perhaps you will think you are in it before it has really begun, and say to yourself, 'Oh! this is really nothing to me. It may be a trial to some, but for me I am sure it is not worth mentioning.' And then, before you know, it will be upon you, and you will fail utterly and shamefully."

"I will be very, very careful," said the princess. "Only don't let me be frightened."

"You shall not be frightened, except it be your own doing. You are already a brave girl, and there is no occasion to try you more that way. I saw how you rushed into the middle of the ugly creatures; and as they ran from you, so will all kinds of evil things, as long as you keep them outside of you, and do not open the cottage of your heart to let them in. I will tell you something more about what you will have to go through.

"Nobody can be a real princess—do not imagine you have yet been anything more than a mock one— until she is a princess over herself, that is, until, when she finds herself unwilling to do the thing that is right, she makes herself do it. So long as any mood she is in makes her do the thing she will be sorry for when that mood is over, she is a slave, and no princess. A princess is able to do what is right even should she unhappily be in a mood that would make another unable to do it. For instance, if you should be cross and angry, you are not a whit the less bound to be just, yes, kind even—a thing most difficult in such a mood—though ease itself in a good mood, loving and sweet. Whoever does what she is bound to do, be she the dirtiest little girl in the street, is a princess, worshipful, honorable. Nay, more; her might goes farther than she could send it, for if she act so, the evil mood will wither and die, and leave her loving and clean.—Do you understand me, dear Rosamond?"

As she spoke, the wise woman laid her hand on her head and looked—oh, so lovingly!—into her eyes.

"I am not sure," said the princess, humbly.

"Perhaps you will understand me better if I say it just comes to this, that you must *not do* what is wrong, however much you are inclined to do it, and you must *do* what is right, however much you are disinclined to do it."

"I understand that," said the princess.

"I am going, then, to put you in one of the mood-chambers of which I have many in the house. Its mood will come upon you, and you will have to deal with it."

She rose and took her by the hand. The princess trembled a little, but never thought of resisting.

The wise woman led her into the great hall with the pictures, and through a door at the farther end, opening upon another large hall, which was circular, and had doors close to each other all round it. Of these she opened one, pushed the princess gently in, and closed it behind her.

The princess found herself in her old nursery. Her little white rabbit came to meet her in a lumping canter as if his back were going to tumble over his head. Her nurse, in her rocking-chair by the chimney corner, sat just as she had used. The fire burned brightly, and on the table were many of her wonderful toys, on which, however, she now looked with some contempt. Her nurse did not seem at all surprised to see her, any more than if the princess had but just gone from the room and returned again.

"Oh! how different I am from what I used to be!" thought the princess to herself, looking from her toys to her nurse. "The wise woman has done me so much good already! I will go and see mamma at once, and tell her I am very glad to be at home again, and very sorry I was so naughty."

She went towards the door.

"Your queen-mamma, princess, cannot see you now," said her nurse.

"I have yet to learn that it is my part to take orders from a servant," said the princess with temper and dignity.

"I beg your pardon, princess," returned her nurse, politely; "but it is my duty to tell you that your queen-mamma is at this moment engaged. She is alone with her most intimate friend, the Princess of the Frozen Regions."

"I shall see for myself," returned the princess, bridling, and walked to the door.

Now little bunny, leap-frogging near the door, happened that moment to get about her feet, just as she was going to open it, so that she tripped and fell against it, striking her forehead a good blow. She caught up the rabbit in a rage, and, crying, "It is all your fault you ugly old wretch!" threw it with violence in her nurse's face.

Her nurse caught the rabbit, and held it to her face, as if seeking to sooth its fright. But the rabbit looked very limp and odd, and, to her amazement, Rosamond presently saw that the thing was no rabbit, but a pocket-handkerchief. The next moment she removed it from her face, and Rosamond beheld—not her nurse, but the wise woman—standing on her own hearth, while she herself stood by the door leading from the cottage into the hall.

"First trial a failure," said the wise woman quietly.

Overcome with shame, Rosamond ran to her, fell down on her knees, and hid her face in her dress.

"Need I say any thing?" said the wise woman, stroking her hair.

"No, no," cried the princess. "I am horrid."

"You know now the kind of thing you have to meet: are you ready to try again?"

"*May* I try again?" cried the princess, jumping up. "I'm ready. I do not think I shall fail this time."

"The trial will be harder."

Rosamond drew in her breath, and set her teeth. The wise woman looked at her pitifully, but took her by the hand, led her to the round hall, opened the same door, and closed it after her.

The princess expected to find herself again in the nursery, but in the wise woman's house no one ever has the same trial twice. She was in a beautiful garden, full of blossoming trees and the loveliest roses and lilies. A lake was in the middle of it, with a tiny boat. So delightful was it that Rosamond forgot all about how or why she had come there, and lost herself in the joy of the flowers and the trees and the water. Presently came the shout of a child, merry and glad, and from a clump of tulip trees rushed a lovely little boy, with his arms stretched out to her. She was charmed at the sight, ran to meet him, caught him up in her arms, kissed him, and could hardly let him go again. But the moment she set him down he ran from her towards the lake, looking back as he ran, and crying "Come, come."

She followed. He made straight for the boat, clambered into it, and held out his hand to help her in. Then he caught up the little boat-hook, and pushed away from the shore: there was a great white flower floating a few yards off, and that was the little fellow's goal. But, alas! no sooner had Rosamond caught sight of it, huge and glowing as a harvest moon, than she felt a great desire to have it herself. The boy, however, was in the bows of the boat, and caught it first. It had a long stem, reaching down to the bottom of the water, and for a moment he tugged at it in vain, but at last it gave way so suddenly, that he tumbled back with the flower into the bottom of the boat. Then Rosamond, almost wild at the danger it was in as he struggled to rise, hurried to save it, but somehow between them it came in pieces, and all its petals of fretted silver were scattered about the boat. When the boy got up, and saw the ruin his companion had occasioned, he burst into tears, and having the long stalk of the flower still in his hand, struck her with it across the face. It did not hurt her much, for he was a very little fellow, but it was wet and slimy. She tumbled rather than rushed at him, seized him in her arms, tore him from his frightened grasp, and flung him into the water. His head struck on the boat as he fell, and he sank at once to the bottom, where he lay looking up at her with white face and open eyes.

The moment she saw the consequences of her deed she was filled with horrible dismay. She tried hard to reach down to him through the water, but it was far deeper than it looked, and she could not. Neither could she get her eyes to leave the white face: its eyes fascinated and fixed hers; and there she lay leaning over the boat and staring at the death she had made. But a voice crying, "Ally! Ally!" shot to her heart, and springing to her feet she saw a lovely lady come running down the grass to the brink of the water with her hair flying about her head.

"Where is my Ally?" she shrieked.

But Rosamond could not answer, and only stared

at the lady, as she had before stared at her drowned boy.

Then the lady caught sight of the dead thing at the bottom of the water, and rushed in, and, plunging down, struggled and groped until she reached it. Then she rose and stood up with the dead body of her little son in her arms, his head hanging back, and the water streaming from him.

"See what you have made of him, Rosamond!" she said, holding the body out to her; "and this is your second trial, and also a failure."

The dead child melted away from her arms, and there she stood, the wise woman, on her own hearth, while Rosamond found herself beside the little well on the floor of the cottage, with one arm wet up to the shoulder. She threw herself on the heather-bed and wept from relief and vexation both.

The wise woman walked out of the cottage, shut the door, and left her alone. Rosamond was sobbing, so that she did not hear her go. When at length she looked up, and saw that the wise woman was gone, her misery returned afresh and tenfold, and she wept and wailed. The hours passed, the shadows of evening began to fall, and the wise woman entered.

XIII

SHE went straight to the bed, and taking Rosamond in her arms, sat down with her by the fire.

"My poor child!" she said. "Two terrible failures! And the more the harder! They get stronger and stronger. What is to be done?"

"Couldn't you help me?" said Rosamond piteously.

"Perhaps I could, now you ask me," answered the wise woman. "When you are ready to try again, we shall see."

"I am very tired of myself," said the princess. "But

87

I can't rest till I try again."

"That is the only way to get rid of your weary, shadowy self, and find your strong, true self. Come, my child; I will help you all I can, for now I *can* help you."

Yet again she led her to the same door, and seemed to the princess to send her yet again alone into the room. She was in a forest, a place half wild, half tended. The trees were grand, and full of the loveliest birds, of all glowing, gleaming and radiant colors, which, unlike the brilliant birds we know in our world, sang deliciously, every one according to his color. The trees were not at all crowded, but their leaves were so thick, and their boughs spread so far, that it was only here and there a sunbeam could get straight through. All the gentle creatures of a forest were there, but no creatures that killed, not even a weasel to kill the rabbits, or a beetle to eat the snails out of their striped shells. As to the butterflies, words would but wrong them if they tried to tell how gorgeous they were. The princess's delight was so great that she neither laughed nor ran, but walked about with a solemn countenance and stately step.

"But where are the flowers?" she said to herself at length.

They were nowhere. Neither on the high trees, nor on the few shrubs that grew here and there amongst them, were there any blossoms; and in the grass that grew everywhere there was not a single flower to be seen.

"Ah, well!" said Rosamond again to herself; "where all the birds and butterflies are living flowers, we can do without the other sort."

Still she could not help feeling that flowers were wanted to make the beauty of the forest complete.

Suddenly she came out on a little open glade; and there, on the root of a great oak, sat the loveliest little girl, with her lap full of flowers of all colors, but of such kinds as Rosamond had never before seen. She was playing with them—burying her hands in them, tumbling them about, and every now and then picking one from the rest, and throwing it away. All the time she never smiled, except with her eyes, which were as full as they could hold of the laughter of the spirit—a laughter which in this world is never heard, only sets the eyes alight with a liquid shining. Rosamond drew nearer, for the wonderful creature would have drawn a tiger to her side, and tamed him on the way. A few yards from her, she came upon one of her cast-away flowers and stooped to pick it up, as well she might where none grew save in her own longing. But to her amazement she found, instead of a flower thrown away to wither, one fast rooted and quite at home. She left it, and went to another; but it also was fast in the soil, and growing comfortably in the warm grass. What could it mean? One after another she tried, until at length she was satisfied that it was the same with every flower the little girl threw from her lap.

She watched then until she saw her throw one, and instantly bounded to the spot. But the flower had been quicker than she: there it grew, fast fixed in the earth, and, she thought, looked at her roguishly. Something evil moved in her, and she plucked it.

"Don't! don't!" cried the child. "My flowers cannot live in your hands."

Rosamond looked at the flower. It was withered already. She threw it from her, offended. The child rose, with difficulty keeping her lapful together, picked it up, carried it back, sat down again, spoke to it, kissed it, sang to it—oh! such a sweet, childish little song!—the princess never could recall a word of it—and threw it away. Up rose its little head, and there it was, busy growing again!

Rosamond's bad temper soon gave way: the beauty and sweetness of the child had overcome it; and, anxious to make friends with her, she drew near, and said:

"Won't you give me a little flower, please, you beautiful child?"

"There they are; they are all for you," answered the child, pointing with her outstretched arm and forefinger all round.

"But you told me, a minute ago, not to touch them."

"Yes, indeed, I did."

"They can't be mine, if I'm not to touch them."

"If, to call them yours, you must kill them, then they are not yours, and never, never can be yours. They are nobody's when they are dead."

"But you don't kill them."

"I don't pull them; I throw them away. I live them."

"How is it that you make them grow?"

"I say, 'You darling!' and throw it away and there it is."

"Where do you get them?"

"In my lap."

"I wish you would let me throw one away."

"Have you got any in your lap? Let me see."

"No; I have none."

"Then you can't throw one away, if you haven't got one."

"You are mocking me!" cried the princess.

"I am not mocking you," said the child, looking her full in the face, with reproach in her large blue eyes.

"Oh, that's where the flowers come from!" said the princess to herself, the moment she saw them, hardly knowing what she meant.

Then the child rose as if hurt, and quickly threw away all the flowers she had in her lap, but one by one, and without any sign of anger. When they were all gone, she stood a moment, and then, in a kind of chanting cry, called, two or three times, "Peggy! Peggy! Peggy!"

A low, glad cry, like the whinny of a horse, answered, and, presently, out of the wood on the opposite side of the glade, came gently trotting the loveliest little snow-white pony, with great shining blue wings, half lifted from his shoulders. Straight towards the little girl, neither hurrying nor lingering, he trotted with light elastic tread.

Rosamond's love for animals broke into a perfect passion of delight at the vision. She rushed to meet the pony with such haste, that, although clearly the best trained animal under the run, he started back, plunged, reared, and struck out with his fore-feet ere he had time to observe what sort of a creature it was that had so startled him. When he perceived it was a little girl, he dropped instantly upon all fours, and content with avoiding her, resumed his quiet trot in the direction of his mistress. Rosamond stood gazing after him in miserable disappointment.

When he reached the child, he laid his head on her shoulder, and she put her arm up round his neck; and after she had talked to him a little, he turned and came trotting back to the princess.

Almost beside herself with joy, she began caressing him in the rough way which, notwithstanding her love for them, she was in the habit of using with animals; and she was not gentle enough, in herself even, to see that he did not like it, and was only putting up with it for the sake of his mistress. But when, that she might jump upon his back, she laid hold of one of his wings and ruffled some of the blue feathers, he wheeled suddenly about, gave his long tail a sharp whisk which threw her flat on the grass, and, trotting back to his mistress, bent down his head before her as if asking excuse for ridding himself of the unbearable.

The princess was furious. She had forgotten all her past life up to the time when she first saw the child: her beauty had made her forget, and yet she was now on the very borders of hating her. What she might have done, or rather tried to do, had not Peggy's tail struck her down with such force that for a moment she could not rise, I cannot tell.

But while she lay half stunned, her eyes fell on a little flower just under them. It stared up in her face like the living thing it was, and she could not take her eyes off its face. It was like a primrose trying to express doubt instead of confidence. It seemed to put her half in mind of something, and she felt as if shame were coming. She put out her hand to pluck it; but the moment her fingers touched it, the flower withered up, and hung as dead on its stalks as if a flame of fire had passed over it.

Then a shudder thrilled through the heart of the princess, and she thought with herself, saying—"What sort of a creature am I that the flowers wither when I touch them, and the ponies despise me with their tails? What a wretched, coarse, ill-bred creature I must be! There is that lovely child given life instead of death to the flowers, and a moment ago I was hating her! I am made horrid, and I shall be horrid, and I hate myself, and yet I can't help being myself!"

She heard the sound of galloping feet, and there was the pony, with the child seated betwixt his wings, coming straight on at full speed for where she lay.

"I don't care," she said. "They may trample me under their feet if they like. I am tired and sick of myself—a creature at whose touch the flowers wither!"

On came the winged pony. But while yet some distance off, he gave a great bound, spread out his living sails of blue, rose yards and yards above her in

The winged pony gave a great bound,
spreading out his living sails of blue.

the air, and alighted as gently as a bird, just a few feet on the other side of her. The child slipped down and came and kneeled over her.

"Did my pony hurt you?" she said. "I am so sorry!"

"Yes, he hurt me," answered the princess, "but not more than I deserved, for I took liberties with him, and he did not like it."

"Oh, you dear!" said the little girl. "I love you for talking so of my Peggy. He is a good pony, though a little playful sometimes. Would you like a ride upon him?"

"You darling beauty!" cried Rosamond, sobbing. "I do love you so, you are so good. How did you become so sweet?"

"Would you like to ride my pony?" repeated the child, with a heavenly smile in her eyes.

"No, no; he is fit only for you. My clumsy body would hurt him," said Rosamond.

"You don't mind me having such a pony?" said the child.

"What! mind it?" cried Rosamond, almost indignantly. Then remembering certain thoughts that had but a few moments before passed through her mind, she looked on the ground and was silent.

"You don't mind it, then?" repeated the child.

"I am very glad there is such a you and such a pony, and that such a you has got such a pony," said Rosamond, still looking on the ground. "But I do wish the flowers would not die when I touch them. I was cross to see you make them grow, but now I should be content if only I did not make them wither."

As she spoke, she stroked the little girl's bare feet, which were by her, half buried in the soft moss, and as she ended she laid her cheek on them and kissed them.

"Dear princess!" said the little girl, "the flowers

will not always wither at your touch. Try now—only do not pluck it. Flowers ought never to be plucked except to give away. Touch it gently."

A silvery flower, something like a snowdrop, grew just within her reach. Timidly she stretched out her hand and touched it. The flower trembled, but neither shrank nor withered.

"Touch it again," said the child.

It changed color a little, and Rosamond fancied it grew larger.

"Touch it again," said the child.

It opened and grew until it was as large as a narcissus, and changed and deepened in color till it was a red glowing gold.

Rosamond gazed motionless. When the transfiguration of the flower was perfected, she sprang to her feet with clasped hands, but for very ecstasy of joy stood speechless, gazing at the child.

"Did you never see me before, Rosamond?" she asked.

"No, never," answered the princess. "I never saw any thing half so lovely."

"Look at me," said the child.

And as Rosamond looked, the child began, like the flower, to grow larger. Quickly through every gradation of growth she passed, until she stood before her a woman perfectly beautiful, neither old nor young; for hers was the old age of everlasting youth.

Rosamond was utterly enchanted, and stood gazing without word or movement until she could endure no more delight. Then her mind collapsed to the thought—had the pony grown too? She glanced round. There was no pony, no grass, no flowers, no bright-birded forest—but the cottage of the wise woman—and before her, on the hearth of it, the goddess-child, the only thing unchanged.

She gasped with astonishment.

"You must set out for your father's palace immediately," said the lady.

"But where is the wise woman?" asked Rosamond, looking all about.

"Here," said the lady.

And Rosamond, looking again, saw the wise woman, folded as usual in her long dark cloak.

"And it was you all the time?" she cried in delight, and kneeled before her, burying her face in her garments.

"It always is me, all the time," said the wise woman, smiling.

"But which is the real you?" asked Rosamond; "this or that?"

"Or a thousand others?" returned the wise woman. "But the one you have just seen is the likest to the real me that you are able to see just yet—but—. And that me you could not have seen a little while ago.—But, my darling child," she went on, lifting her up and clasping her to her bosom, "you must not think, because you have seen me once, that therefore you are capable of seeing me at all times. No; there are many things in you yet that must be changed before that can be. Now, however, you will seek me. Every time you feel you want me, that is a sign I am wanting you. There are yet many rooms in my house you may have to go through; but when you need no more of them, then you will be able to throw flowers like the little girl you saw in the forest."

The princess gave a sigh.

"Do you think," the wise woman went on, "that the things you have seen in my house are mere empty shows. You do not know, you cannot yet think, how living and true they are.—Now you must go."

She led her once more into the great hall, and there showed her the picture of her father's capital, and his palace with the brazen gates.

"There is your home," she said "Go to it."

The princess understood, and a flush of shame rose to her forehead. She turned to the wise woman and said:

"Will you forgive *all* my naughtiness, and *all* the trouble I have given you?"

"If I had not forgiven you, I would never have taken the trouble to punish you. If I had not loved you, do you think I would have carried you away in my cloak?"

"How could you love such an ugly, ill-tempered, rude, hateful little wretch?"

"I saw, through it all, what you were going to be," said the wise woman, kissing her. "But remember you have yet only *begun* to be what I saw."

"I will try to remember," said the princess, holding her cloak, and looking up in her face.

"Go, then," said the wise woman.

Rosamond turned away on the instant, ran to the picture, stepped over the frame of it, heard a door close gently, gave one glance back, saw behind her the loveliest palace-front of alabaster, gleaming in the pale-yellow light of an early summer-morning, looked again to the eastward, saw the faint outline of her father's city against the sky, and ran off to reach it.

It looked much further off now than when it seemed a picture, but the sun was not yet up, and she had the whole of a summer day before her.

XIV

THE soldiers sent out by the king, had no great difficulty in finding Agnes's father and mother, of whom they demanded if they knew any thing of such a young princess as they described. The honest pair told them the truth in every point—that, having lost their own child and found another, they had taken her home, and treated her as their own; that she had indeed called herself a princess, but they had not believed her, because she did not look like one; that, even if they had, they did not know how they could have done differently, seeing they were poor people who could not afford to keep any idle person about the place; that they had done their best to teach her good ways, and had not parted with her until her bad temper rendered it impossible to put up with her any longer; that, as to the king's proclamation, they heard little of the world's news on their lonely hill, and it had never reached them; that if it had, they did not know how either of them could have gone such a distance from home, and left their sheep or their cottage, one or the other, uncared for.

"You must learn, then, how both of you can go, and your sheep must take care of your cottage," said the lawyer, and commanded the soldier to bind them hand and foot.

Heedless of their entreaties to be spared such an indignity, the soldiers obeyed, bore them to a cart, and set out for the king's palace, leaving the cottage door open, the fire burning, the pot of potatoes boiling upon it, the sheep scattered over the hill, and the dogs not knowing what to do.

Hardly were they gone, however, before the wise woman walked up, with Prince behind her, peeped into the cottage, locked the door, put the key in her pocket, and then walked away up the hill. In a few minutes there arose a great battle between Prince and the dog which filled his former place—a well-meaning but dull fellow, who could fight better than feed. Prince was not long in showing him that he was meant for his master, and then, by his effort, and directions to the other dogs, the sheep were soon gathered again, and out of danger from foxes and bad dogs. As soon as this was done, the wise woman left them in charge of Prince, while she went to the next farm to arrange for the folding of the sheep and the feeding of the dogs.

When the soldiers reached the palace, they were ordered to carry their prisoners at once into the presence of the king and queen, in the throne room. Their two thrones stood upon a high dais at one end, and on the floor at the foot of the dais, the soldiers laid their helpless prisoners. The queen commanded that they should be unbound, and ordered them to stand up. They obeyed with the dignity of insulted innocence, and their bearing offended their foolish majesties.

Meantime the princess, after a long day's journey, arrived at the palace, and walked up to the sentry at the gate.

"Stand back," said the sentry.

"I wish to go in, if you please," said the princess gently.

"Ha! ha! ha!" laughed the sentry, for he was one of those dull people who form their judgment from a person's clothes, without even looking in his eyes; and as the princess happened to be in rags, her request was amusing, and the booby thought himself quite clever for laughing at her so thoroughly.

"I am the princess," Rosamond said quietly.

"*What* princess?" bellowed the man.

"The princess Rosamond. Is there another?" she answered and asked.

But the man was so tickled at the wonderous idea of a princess in rags, that he scarcely heard what she said for laughing. As soon as he recovered a little, he proceeded to chuck the princess under the chin, saying—

"You're a pretty girl, my dear, though you ain't no princess."

Rosamond drew back with dignity.

"You have spoken three untruths at once," she said. "I am *not* pretty, and I *am* a princess, and if I were dear to you, as I ought to be, you would not laugh at me because I am badly dressed, but stand aside, and let me to my father and mother."

The tone of her speech, and the rebuke she gave him, made the man look at her; and looking at her, he began to tremble inside his foolish body, and wonder whether he might not have made a mistake. He raised his hand in salute, and said—

"I beg your pardon, miss, but I have express orders to admit no child whatever within the palace gates. They tell me his majesty the king says he is sick of children."

"He may well be sick of me!" thought the princess; "but it can't mean that he does not want me home again.—I don't think you can very well call me a child," she said, looking the sentry full in the face.

"You ain't very big, miss," answered the soldier, "but so be you say you ain't a child, I'll take the risk. The king can only kill me, and a man must die once."

He opened the gate, stepped aside, and allowed her to pass. Had she lost her temper, as every one but the wise woman would have expected of her, he certainly would not have done so.

She ran into the palace, the door of which had been left open by the porter when he followed the soldiers and prisoners to the throne-room and bounded up the stairs to look for her father and mother. As she passed the door of the throne-room she heard an unusual noise in it, and running to the king's private entrance, over which hung a heavy curtain, she peeped past the edge of it, and saw, to her amazement, the shepherd and shepherdess standing like culprits before the king and queen, and the same moment heard the king say—

"Peasants, where is the princess Rosamond?"

"Truly, sire, we do not know," answered the shepherd.

"You ought to know," said the king.

"Sire, we could keep her no longer."

"You confess, then," said the king suppressing the outbreak of the wrath that boiled up in him, "that you turned her out of your house."

For the king had been informed by a swift messenger of all that had passed long before the arrival of the prisoners.

"We did, sire; but not only could we keep her no longer, but we knew not that she was the princess."

"You ought to have known, the moment you cast your eyes upon her," said the king. "Any one who does not know a princess the moment he sees her, ought to have his eyes put out."

"Indeed he ought," said the queen.

To this they returned no answer, for they had none ready.

"Why did you not bring her at once to the palace," pursued the king, "whether you knew her to be a princess or not? My proclamation left nothing to your judgment. It said *every child*."

"We heard nothing of the proclamation, sire."

"You ought to have heard," said the king. "It is enough that I make proclamations; it is for you to read them. Are they not written in letters of gold upon the brazen gates of this palace?"

"A poor shepherd, your majesty—how often must he leave his flock, and go hundreds of miles to look whether there may not be something in letters of gold upon the brazen gates? We did not know that your majesty had made a proclamation, or even that the princess was lost."

"You ought to have known," said the king.

The shepherd held his peace.

101

"But," said the queen, taking up the word, "all this is as nothing, when I think how you misused the darling."

The only ground the queen had for saying thus, was what Agnes had told her as to how the princess was dressed; and her condition seemed to the queen so miserable, that she had imagined all sorts of oppression and cruelty.

But this was more than the shepherdess, who had not yet spoken, could bear.

"She would have been dead, and *not* buried, long ago, madam, if I had not carried her home in my two arms."

"Why does she say her *two* arms?" said the king to himself. "Has she more than two? Is there treason in that?"

"You dressed her in cast-off clothes," said the queen.

"I dressed her in my own sweet child's Sunday clothes. And this is what I get for it!" cried the shepherdess, bursting into tears.

"And what did you do with the clothes you took off her? Sell them?"

"Put them in the fire, madam. They were not fit for the poorest child in the mountains. They were so ragged that you could see her skin through them in twenty different places."

"You cruel woman, to torture a mother's feelings so!" cried the queen, and in her turn burst into tears.

"And I'm sure," sobbed the shepherdess, "I took every pains to teach her what it was right for her to know. I taught her to tidy the house, and"—

"Tidy the house?" moaned the queen. "My poor wretched offspring!"

"And peel the potatoes, and"—

"Peel the potatoes!" cried the queen. "Oh, horror!"

"And black her master's boots, said the shepherdess.

"Black her master's boots!" shrieked the queen. "Oh, my white-handed princess! Oh, my ruined baby!"

"What I want to know," said the king, paying no heed to this maternal duel, but patting the top of his sceptre as if it had been the hilt of a sword which he was about to draw, "is, where the princess is now."

The shepherd made no answer, for he had nothing to say more than he had said already.

"You have murdered her!" shouted the king. "You shall be tortured till you confess the truth; and then you shall be tortured to death, for you are the most abominable wretches in the whole wide world."

"Who accuses me of crime?" cried the shepherd, indignant.

"I accuse you," said the king: "but you shall see, face to face, the chief witness to your villainy. Officer, bring the girl."

Silence filled the hall while they waited. The king's face was swollen with anger. The queen hid hers behind her handkerchief. The shepherd and shepherdess bent their eyes on the ground, wondering. It was with difficulty Rosamond could keep her place, but so wise had she already become that she saw it would be far better to let every thing come out before she interfered.

At length the door opened, and in came the officer, followed by Agnes, looking white as death and mean as sin.

The shepherdess gave a shriek, and darted towards her with arms spread wide; the shepherd followed, but not so eagerly.

"My child! my lost darling! my Agnes!" cried the shepherdess.

"Hold them asunder," shouted the king. "Here is

more villainy! What! have I a scullery-maid in my house born of such parents? The parents of such a child must be capable of any thing. Take all three of them to the rack. Stretch them till their joints are torn asunder, and give them no water. Away with them!"

The soldiers approached to lay hands on them. But, behold! a girl all in rags, with such a radiant countenance that it was right lovely to see, darted between, and careless of the royal presence, flung herself upon the shepherdess, crying,—

"Do not touch her. She is my good, kind mistress."

But the shepherdess could hear or see no one but her Agnes, and pushed her away. Then the princess turned, with the tears in her eyes, to the shepherd, and threw her arms about his neck and pulled down his head and kissed him. And the tall shepherd lifted her to his bosom and kept her there, but his eyes were fixed on his Agnes.

"What is the meaning of this?" cried the king, starting up from his throne. "How did that ragged girl get in here? Take her away with the rest. She is one of them, too."

But the princess made the shepherd set her down, and before any one could interfere she had run up the steps of the dais and then the steps of the king's throne like a squirrel, flung herself upon the king, and begun to smother him with kisses.

All stood astonished, except the three peasants, who did not even see what took place. The shepherdess kept calling to her Agnes, but she was so ashamed that she did not dare even lift her eyes to meet her mother's, and the shepherd kept gazing on her in silence. As for the king, he was so breathless and aghast with astonishment, that he was too feeble to fling the ragged child from him, as he tried to do. But she left him, and running down the steps of the one throne and up those of the other, began kissing the queen next. But the queen cried out,—

"Get away, you great rude child!—Will nobody take her to the rack?"

Then the princess, hardly knowing what she did for joy that she had come in time, ran down the steps of the throne and the dais, and placing herself between the shepherd and shepherdess, took a hand of each, and stood looking at the king and queen.

Their faces began to change. At last they began to know her. But she was so altered—so lovelily altered, that it was no wonder they should not have known her at the first glance; but it was the fault of the pride and anger and injustice with which their hearts were filled, that they did not know her at the second.

The king gazed and the queen gazed, both half risen from their thrones, and looking as if about to tumble down upon her, if only they could be right sure that the ragged girl was their own child. A mistake would be such a dreadful thing!

"My darling!" at last shrieked the mother, a little doubtfully.

"My pet of pets?" cried the father, with an interrogative twist of tone.

Another moment, and they were half-way down the steps of the dais.

"Stop!" said the voice of command from somewhere in the hall, and, king and queen as they were, they stopped at once half-way, then drew themselves up, stared, and began to grow angry again, but durst not go farther.

The wise woman was coming slowly up through the crowd that filled the hall. Every one made way for her. She came straight on until she stood in front of the king and queen.

"Miserable man and woman!" she said, in words they alone could hear, "I took your daughter away when she was worthy of such parents; I bring her back, and they are unworthy of her. That you did not know her when she came to you is a small wonder, for you have been blind in soul all your lives: now be blind in body until your better eyes are unsealed."

She threw her cloak open. It fell to the ground, and the radiance that flashed from her robe of snowy whiteness, from her face of awful beauty, and from her eyes that shone like pools of sunlight, smote them blind.

Rosamond saw them give a great start, shudder, waver to and fro, then sit down on the steps of the dais; and she knew they were punished, but knew not how. She rushed up to them, and catching a hand of each said—

"Father, dear father! mother dear! I will ask the wise woman to forgive you."

"Oh, I am blind! I am blind!" they cried together. "Dark as night! Stone blind!"

Rosamond left them, sprang down the steps, and kneeling at her feet, cried, "Oh, my lovely wise woman! do let them see. Do open their eyes, dear, good, wise woman."

The wise woman bent down to her, and said, so that none else could hear,

"I will one day. Meanwhile you must be their servant, as I have been yours. Bring them to me, and I will make them welcome."

Rosamond rose, went up the steps again to her father and mother, where they sat like statues with closed eyes, half-way from the top of the dais where stood their empty thrones, seated herself between them, took a hand of each, and was still.

All this time very few in the room saw the wise woman. The moment she threw off her cloak she vanished from the sight of almost all who were present. The woman who swept and dusted the hall and brushed the thrones, saw her, and the shepherd had a glimmering vision of her; but no one else that I know of caught a glimpse of her. The shepherdess did not see her. Nor did Agnes, but she felt the presence upon her like the heat of a furnace seven times heated.

As soon as Rosamond had taken her place between her father and mother, the wise woman lifted her cloak from the floor, and threw it again around her. Then everybody saw her, and Agnes felt as if a soft dewy cloud had come between her and the torrid rays of a vertical sun. The wise woman turned to the shepherd and shepherdess.

"For you," she said, "you are sufficiently punished by the work of your own hands. Instead of making your daughter obey you, you left her to be a slave to herself; you coaxed when you ought to have compelled; you praised when you ought to have been silent; you fondled when you ought to have punished; you threatened when you ought to have inflicted—and there she stands, the full-grown result of your foolishness! She is your crime and your punishment. Take her home with you, and live hour after hour with the pale-heated disgrace you call your daughter. What she is, the worm at her heart has begun to teach her. When life is no longer endurable, come to me.

"Madam," said the shepherd, "may I not go with you now?"

"You shall," said the wise woman.

"Husband! husband!" cried the shepherdess, "how are we two to get home without you?"

"I will see to that," said the wise woman. "But little of home you will find it until you have come to me. The king carried you hither, and he shall carry you back. But your husband shall not go with you. He cannot now if he would."

The shepherdess looked and saw that the shepherd stood in a deep sleep. She went to him and sought to rouse him, but neither tongue nor hands were of the slightest avail.

The wise woman turned to Rosamond.

"My child," she said, "I shall never be far from you. Come to me when you will. Bring them to me."

Rosamond smiled and kissed her hand, but kept her place by her parents. They also were now in a deep sleep like the shepherd.

The wise woman took the shepherd by the hand, and led him away.

And that is all my double story. How double it is, if you care to know, you must find out. If you think it is not finished—I never knew a story that was. I could tell you a great deal more concerning them all, but I have already told more than is good for those who read but with their foreheads, and enough for those whom it has made look a little solemn, and sigh as they close the book.

LITTLE DAYLIGHT

NO house of any pretension to be called a palace is in the least worthy of the name, except it has a wood near it—very near it—and the nearer the better. Not all round it—I don't mean that, for a palace ought to be open to the sun and wind, and stand high and brave, with weathercocks glittering and flags flying; but on one side of every palace there must be a wood. And there was a very grand wood indeed beside the palace of the king who was going to be Daylight's father; such a grand wood, that nobody yet had ever got to the other end of it. Near the house it was kept very trim and nice, and it was free of brushwood for a long way in; but by degrees it got wild, and it grew wilder, and wilder, and wilder, until some said wild beasts at last did what they liked in it. The king and his courtiers often hunted, however, and this kept the wild beasts far away from the palace.

One glorious summer morning, when the wind and sun were out together, when the vanes were flashing and the flags frolicking against the blue sky, little Daylight made her appearance from somewhere—nobody could tell where—a beautiful baby, with such bright eyes that she might have come from the sun, only by and by she showed such lively ways that she might equally well have come out of the wind. There was great jubilation in the palace, for

Reprinted from *Works of Fancy and Imagination* (1871).

this was the first baby the queen had had, and there is as much happiness over a new baby in a palace as in a cottage.

But there is one disadvantage of living near a wood: you do not know quite who your neighbours may be. Everybody knew there were in it several fairies, living within a few miles of the palace, who always had had something to do with each new baby that came; for fairies live so much longer than we, that they can have business with a good many generations of human mortals. The curious houses they lived in were well known also,—one, a hollow oak; another, a birch-tree, though nobody could ever find how that fairy made a house of it; another, a hut of growing trees intertwined, and patched up with turf and moss. But there was another fairy who had lately come to the place, and nobody even knew she was a fairy except the other fairies. A wicked old thing she was, always concealing her power, and being as disagreeable as she could, in order to tempt people to give her offence, that she might have the pleasure of taking vengeance upon them. The people about thought she was a witch, and those who knew her by sight were careful to avoid offending her. She lived in a mud house, in a swampy part of the forest.

In all history we find that fairies give their remarkable gifts to prince or princess, or any child of sufficient importance in their eyes, always at the christening. Now this we can understand, because it is an ancient custom amongst human beings as well; and it is not hard to explain why wicked fairies should choose the same time to do unkind things; but it is difficult to understand how they should be able to do them, for you would fancy all wicked creatures would be powerless on such an occasion. But I never knew of any interference on the part of a wicked fairy that did not turn out a good thing in the end. What a good thing, for instance, it was that one princess should sleep for a hundred years! Was she not saved from all the plague of young men who were not worthy of her? And did she not come awake exactly at the right moment when the right prince kissed her? For my part, I cannot help wishing a good many girls would sleep till just the same fate overtook them. It would be happier for them, and more agreeable to their friends.

Of course all the known fairies were invited to the christening. But the king and queen never thought of inviting an old witch. For the power of the fairies they have by nature; whereas a witch gets her power by wickedness. The other fairies, however, knowing the danger thus run, provided as well as they could against accidents from her quarter. But they could neither render her powerless, nor could they arrange their gifts in reference to hers beforehand, for they could not tell what those might be.

Of course the old hag was there without being asked. Not to be asked was just what she wanted, that she might have a sort of a reason for doing what she wished to do. For somehow even the wickedest of creatures likes a pretext for doing the wrong thing.

Five fairies had one after the other given the child such gifts as each counted best, and the fifth had just stepped back to her place in the surrounding splendour of ladies and gentlemen, when, mumbling a laugh between her toothless gums, the wicked fairy hobbled out into the middle of the circle, and at the moment when the archbishop was handing the baby to the lady at the head of the nursery department of state affairs, addressed him thus, giving a bite or two to every word before she could part with it:

"Please your Grace, I'm very deaf: would your Grace mind repeating the princess's name?"

"With pleasure, my good woman," said the archbishop, stooping to shout in her ear: "the infant's name is little Daylight."

"And little daylight it shall be," cried the fairy, in the tone of a dry axle, "and little good shall any of her gifts do her. For I bestow upon her the gift of sleeping all day long, whether she will or not. Ha, ha! He, he! Hi, hi!"

Then out started the sixth fairy, who, of course, the others had arranged should come after the wicked one, in order to undo as much as she might.

"If she sleep all day," she said mournfully, "she shall, at least, wake all night."

"A nice prospect for her mother and me!" thought the poor king; for they loved her far too much to give her up to nurses, especially at night, as most kings and queens do—and are sorry for it afterwards.

"You spoke before I had done," said the wicked fairy. "That's against the law. It gives me another chance."

"I beg your pardon," said the other fairies, all together.

"She did. I hadn't done laughing," said the crone. "I had only got to Hi, hi! and I had to go through Ho, ho! and Hu, hu! So I decree that if she wakes all night she shall wax and wane with its mistress the moon. And what that may mean I hope her royal parents will live to see. Ho, ho! Hu, hu!"

But out stepped another fairy, for they had been wise enough to keep two in reserve, because every fairy knew the trick of one.

"Until," said the seventh fairy, "a prince comes who shall kiss her without knowing it."

The wicked fairy made a horrid noise like an angry cat, and hobbled away. She could not pretend that she had not finished her speech this time, for she had laughed Ho, ho! and Hu, hu!

"I don't know what that means," said the poor king to the seventh fairy.

"Don't be afraid. The meaning will come with the thing itself," said she.

The assembly broke up, miserable enough—the queen, at least, prepared for a good many sleepless nights, and the lady at the head of the nursery department anything but comfortable in the prospect

113

before her, for of course the queen could not do it all. As for the king, he made up his mind, with what courage he could summon, to meet the demands of the case, but wondered whether he could with any propriety require the First Lord of the Treasury to take a share in the burden laid upon him.

I will not attempt to describe what they had to go through for some time. But at last the household settled into a regular system—a very irregular one in some respects. For at certain seasons the palace rang all night with bursts of laughter from little Daylight, whose heart the old fairy's curse could not reach; she was Daylight still, only a little in the wrong place, for she always dropped asleep at the first hint of dawn in the east. But her merriment was of short duration. When the moon was at the full, she was in glorious spirits, and as beautiful as it was possible for a child of her age to be. But as the moon waned, she faded, until at last she was wan and withered like the poorest, sickliest child you might come upon in the streets of a great city in the arms of a homeless mother. Then the night was quiet as the day, for the little creature lay in her gorgeous cradle night and day with hardly a motion, and indeed at last without even a moan, like one dead. At first they often thought she was dead, but at last they got used to it, and only consulted the almanac to find the moment when she would begin to revive, which, of course, was with the first appearance of the silver thread of the crescent moon. Then she would move her lips, and they would give her a little nourishment; and she would grow better and better and better, until for a few days she was spendidly well. When well, she was always merriest out in the moonlight; but even when near her worst, she seemed better when, in warm summer nights, they carried her cradle out into the light of the waning moon. Then in her sleep she would smile the faintest, most pitiful smile.

For a long time very few people ever saw her awake. As she grew older she became such a favourite, however, that about the palace there were always some who would contrive to keep awake at night, in order to be near her. But she soon began to take every chance of getting away from her nurses and enjoying her moonlight alone. And thus things went on until she was nearly seventeen years of age. Her father and mother had by that time got so used to the odd state of things that they had ceased to wonder at them. All their arrangements had reference to the state of the Princess Daylight, and it is amazing how things contrive to accommodate themselves. But how any prince was ever to find and deliver her, appeared inconceivable.

As she grew older she had grown more and more beautiful, with the sunniest hair and the loveliest eyes of heavenly blue, brilliant and profound as the sky of a June day. But so much more painful and sad was the change as her bad time came on. The more beautiful she was in the full moon, the more withered and worn did she become as the moon waned. At the time at which my story has now arrived, she looked, when the moon was small or gone, like an old woman exhausted with suffering. This was the more painful that her appearance was unnatural; for her hair and eyes did not change. Her wan face was both drawn and wrinkled, and had an eager hungry look. Her skinny hands moved as if wishing, but unable, to lay hold of something. Her shoulders were bent forward, her chest went in, and she stooped as if she were eighty years old. At last she had to be put to bed, and there await the flow of the tide of life. But she grew to dislike being seen, still more being touched by any hands, during this season. One lovely summer evening, when the moon lay all but gone upon the verge of the horizon, she vanished from her attendants, and it was only after searching for her a long time in great terror, that they found her fast asleep in the forest, at the foot of a silver birch, and carried her home.

A little way from the palace there was a great open glade, covered with the greenest and softest grass. This was her favourite haunt; for here the full moon shone free and glorious, while through a vista in the trees she could generally see more or less of the dying moon as it crossed the opening. Here she had a little rustic house built for her, and here she mostly resided. None of the court might go there without leave, and her own attendants had learned by this time not to be officious in waiting upon her, so that she was very much at liberty. Whether the good fairies had anything to do with it or not I cannot tell, but at last she got into the way of retreating further into the wood every night as the moon waned, so that sometimes they had great trouble in finding her; but as she was always very angry if she discovered they were watching her, they scarcely dared to do so. At length one night they thought they had lost her altogether. It was morning before they found her. Feeble as she was, she had wandered into a thicket a long way from the glade, and there she lay—fast asleep, of course.

Although the fame of her beauty and sweetness had gone abroad, yet as everybody knew she was under a bad spell, no king in the neighbourhood had any desire to have her for a daughter-in-law. There were serious objections to such a relation.

About this time in a neighbouring kingdom, in consequence of the wickedness of the nobles, an insurrection took place upon the death of the old king, the greater part of the nobility was massacred, and the young prince was compelled to flee for his life, disguised like a peasant. For some time, until he got out of the country, he suffered much from hunger and fatigue; but when he got into that ruled by the princess's father, and had no longer any fear of being recognized, he fared better, for the people were kind. He did not abandon his disguise, however. One tolerable reason was that he had no other clothes to put on, and another that he had very little money, and did not know where to get any more. There was no good in telling everybody he met that he was a prince, for he felt that a prince ought to be able to get on like other people, else his rank only made a fool of him. He had read of princes setting out upon adventure; and here he was out in similar case, only without having had a choice in the matter. He would go on, and see what would come of it.

For a day or two he had been walking through the palace-wood, and had had next to nothing to eat, when he came upon the strangest little house, inhabited by a very nice tidy motherly old woman. This was one of the good fairies. The moment she saw him she knew quite well who he was and what was going to come of it; but she was not at liberty to interfere with the orderly march of events. She received him with the kindness she would have shown to any other traveller, and gave him bread and milk, which he thought the most delicious food he had ever tasted, wondering that they did not have it for dinner at the palace sometimes. The old woman pressed him to stay all night. When he awoke he was amazed to find how well and strong he felt. She would not take any of the money he offered, but begged him, if he found occasion of continuing in the neighbourhood, to return and occupy the same quarters.

"Thank you much, good mother," answered the prince; "but there is little chance of that. The sooner I get out of this wood the better."

"I don't know that," said the fairy.

"What do you mean?" asked the prince.

"Why how *should* I know?" returned she.

"I can't tell," said the prince.

"Very well," said the fairy.

"How strangely you talk!" said the prince.

"Do I?" said the fairy.

"Yes, you do," said the prince.

"Very well," said the fairy.

The prince was not used to being spoken to in this fashion, so he felt a little angry and turned and walked away. But this did not offend the fairy. She stood at the door of her little house looking after him till the trees hid him quite. Then she said "At last!" and went in.

The prince wandered and wandered, and got nowhere. The sun sank and sank and went out of sight, and he seemed no nearer the end of the wood than ever. He sat down on a fallen tree, ate a bit of bread the old woman had given him, and waited for the moon; for, although he was not much of an astronomer, he knew the moon would rise some time, because she had risen the night before. Up she came, slow and slow, but of a good size, pretty nearly round indeed; whereupon, greatly refreshed with his piece of bread, he got up and went—he knew not whither.

After walking a considerable distance, he thought he was coming to the outside of the forest; but when he reached what he thought the last of it, he found himself only upon the edge of a great open space in it, covered with grass. The moon shone very bright, and he thought he had never seen a more lovely spot. Still it looked dreary because of its loneliness, for he could not see the house at the other side. He sat down weary again, and gazed into the glade. He had not seen so much room for several days.

All at once he espied something in the middle of the grass. What could it be? It moved; it came nearer.

118

Was it a human creature, gliding across—a girl dressed in white, gleaming in the moonshine? She came nearer and nearer. He crept behind a tree and watched, wondering. It must be some strange being of the wood—a nymph whom the moonlight and the warm dusky air had enticed from her tree. But when she came close to where he stood, he no longer doubted she was human—for he had caught sight of her sunny hair, and her clear blue eyes, and the loveliest face and form that he had ever seen. All at once she began singing like a nightingale, and dancing to her own music, with her eyes ever turned towards the moon. She passed close to where he stood, dancing on by the edge of the trees and away in a great circle towards the other side, until he could see but a spot of white in the yellowish green of the moonlit grass. But when he feared it would vanish quite, the spot grew, and became a figure once more. She approached him again, singing and dancing and waving her arms over her head, until she had completed the circle. Just opposite his tree she stood, ceased her song, dropped her arms, and broke out into a long clear laugh, musical as a brook. Then, as if tired, she threw herself on the grass, and lay gazing at the moon. The prince was almost afraid to breathe lest he should startle her, and she should vanish from his sight. As to venturing near her, that never came into his head.

She had lain for a long hour or longer, when the prince began again to doubt concerning her. Perhaps she was but a vision of his own fancy. Or was she a spirit of the wood, after all? If so, he too would haunt the wood, glad to have lost kingdom and everything for the hope of being near her. He would build him a hut in the forest, and there he would live for the pure chance of seeing her again. Upon nights like this at least she would come out and bask in the moonlight, and make his soul blessed. But while he thus

119

Little Daylight danced to her own music,
passing close to where the prince stood.

dreamed she sprang to her feet, turned her face full to the moon, and began singing as if she would draw her down from the sky by the power of her entrancing voice. She looked more beautiful than ever. Again she began dancing to her own music, and danced away into the distance. Once more she returned in a similar manner; but although he was watching as eagerly as before, what with fatigue and what with gazing, he fell fast asleep before she came near him. When he awoke it was broad daylight, and the princess was nowhere.

He could not leave the place. What if she should come the next night! He would gladly endure a day's hunger to see her yet again: he would buckle his belt quite tight. He walked round the glade to see if he could discover any prints of her feet. But the grass was so short, and her steps had been so light, that she had not left a single trace behind her.

He walked half-way round the wood without seeing anything to account for her presence. Then he spied a lovely little house, with thatched roof and low eaves, surrounded by an exquisite garden, with doves and peacocks walking in it. Of course this must be where the gracious lady who loved the moonlight lived. Forgetting his appearance, he walked towards the door, determined to make inquiries, but as he passed a little pond full of gold and silver fishes, he caught sight of himself, and turned to find the door to the kitchen. There he knocked, and asked for a piece of bread. The good-natured cook brought him in, and gave him an excellent breakfast, which the prince found nothing the worse for being served in the kitchen. While he ate, he talked with his entertainer, and learned that this was the favourite retreat of the Princess Daylight. But he learned nothing more, both because he was afraid of seeming inquisitive, and because the cook did not choose to be heard talking about her mistress to a peasant lad who had begged for his breakfast.

As he rose to take his leave, it occurred to him that he might not be so far from the old woman's cottage as he had thought, and he asked the cook whether she knew anything of such a place, describing it as well as he could. She said she knew it well enough, adding with a smile—

"It's there you're going, is it?"

"Yes, if it's not far off."

"It's not more than three miles. But mind what you are about, you know."

"Why do you say that?"

"If you're after any mischief, she'll make you repent it."

"The best thing that could happen under the circumstances," remarked the prince.

"What do you mean by that?" asked the cook.

"Why, it stands to reason," answered the prince, "that if you wish to do anything wrong, the best thing for you is to be made to repent of it."

"I see," said the cook. "Well, I think you may venture. She's a good old soul."

"Which way does it lie from here?" asked the prince.

She gave him full instructions; and he left her with many thanks.

Being now refreshed, however, the prince did not go back to the cottage that day: he remained in the forest, amusing himself as best he could, but awaiting anxiously for the night, in the hope that the princess would again appear. Nor was he disappointed, for, directly the moon rose, he spied a glimmering shape far across the glade. As it drew nearer, he saw it was she indeed—not dressed in white as before: in a pale blue like the sky, she looked lovelier still. He thought it was that the blue suited her yet better than the white; he did not know that she was really more beautiful because the moon was nearer the full. In fact the next night was full moon, and the princess would then be at the zenith of her loveliness.

The prince feared for some time that she was not coming near his hiding-place that night; but the circles in her dance ever widened as the moon rose, until at last they embraced the whole glade, and she came still closer to the trees where he was hiding than she had come the night before. He was entranced with her loveliness, for it was indeed a marvellous thing. All night long he watched her, but dared not go near her. He would have been ashamed of watching her too, had he not become almost incapable of thinking of anything but how beautiful she was. He watched the whole night long, and saw that as the moon went down she retreated in smaller and smaller circles, until at last he could see her no more.

Weary as he was, he set out for the old woman's cottage, where he arrived just in time for her breakfast, which she shared with him. He then went to bed, and slept for many hours. When he awoke, the sun was down, and he departed in great anxiety lest he should lose a glimpse of the lovely vision. But, whether it was by the machinations of the swamp-fairy, or merely that it is one thing to go and another to return by the same road, he lost his way. I shall not attempt to describe his misery when the moon rose, and he saw nothing but trees, trees, trees. She was high in the heavens before he reached the glade. Then indeed his troubles vanished, for there was the princess coming dancing towards him, in a dress that shone like gold, and with shoes that glimmered through the grass like fire-flies. She was of course still more beautiful than before. Like an embodied sunbeam she passed him, and danced away into the distance.

Before she returned in her circle, clouds had begun to gather about the moon. The wind rose, the trees moaned, and their lighter branches leaned all one way before it. The prince feared that the princess would go in, and he should see her no more that night. But she came dancing on more jubilant than ever, her golden dress and her sunny hair streaming out upon the blast, waving her arms towards the moon, and in the exuberance of her delight ordering the clouds away from off her face. The prince could hardly believe she was not a creature of the elements, after all.

By the time she had completed another circle, the clouds had gathered deep, and there were growlings of distant thunder. Just as she passed the tree where he stood, a flash of lightning blinded him for a moment, and when he saw again, to his horror, the princess lay on the ground. He darted to her, thinking she had been struck; but when she heard him coming, she was on her feet in a moment.

"What do you want?" she asked.

"I beg your pardon. I thought—the lightning—" said the prince, hesitating.

"There is nothing the matter," said the princess, waving him off rather haughtily.

The poor prince turned and walked towards the wood.

"Come back," said Daylight; "I like you. You do what you are told. Are you good?"

"Not so good as I should like to be," said the prince.

"Then go and grow better," said the princess.

Again the disappointed prince turned and went.

"Come back," said the princess.

He obeyed, and stood before her waiting.

"Can you tell me what the sun is like?" she asked.

"No," he answered. "But where's the good of asking what you know?"

"But I don't know," she rejoined.

"Why, everybody knows."

"That's the very thing: I'm not everybody. I've never seen the sun."

"Then you can't know what it's like till you do see it."

"I think you must be a prince," said the princess.

"Do I look like one?" said the prince.

"I can't quite say that."

"Then why do you think so?"

"Because you both do what you are told and speak the truth.—Is the sun so very bright?"

"As bright as the lightning."

"But it doesn't go out like that, does it?"

"Oh no. It shines like the moon, rises and sets like the moon, is much the same shape as the moon, only so bright that you can't look at it for a moment."

"But I *would* look at it," said the princess.

"But you couldn't," said the prince.

"But I could," said the princess.

"Why don't you, then?"

"Because I can't."

"Why can't you?"

"Because I can't wake. And I never shall wake until—"

Here she hid her face in her hands, turned away, and walked in the slowest, stateliest manner towards the house. The prince ventured to follow her at a little distance, but she turned and made a repellent gesture, which, like a true gentleman-prince, he obeyed at once. He waited a long time, but as she did not come near him again, and as the night had now cleared, he set off at last for the old woman's cottage.

It was long past midnight when he reached it, but, to his surprise, the old woman was paring potatoes at the door. Fairies are fond of doing odd things. Indeed, however they may dissemble, the night is always their day. And so it is with all who have fairy blood in them.

"Why, what are you doing there, this time of the night, mother?" said the prince; for that was the kind way in which any young man in his country would address a woman who was much older than himself.

"Getting your supper ready, my son," she answered.

"Oh! I don't want any supper," said the prince.

"Ah! you've seen Daylight," said she.

"I've seen a princess who never saw it," said the prince.

"Do you like her?" asked the fairy.

"Oh! don't I?" said the prince. "More than you would believe, mother."

"A fairy can believe anything that ever was or ever could be," said the old woman.

"Then are you a fairy?" asked the prince.

"Yes," said she.

"Then what do you do for things not to believe?" asked the prince.

"There's plenty of them—everything that never was nor ever could be."

"Plenty, I grant you," said the prince. "But do you believe there could be a princess who never saw the daylight? Do you believe that, now?"

This the prince said, not that he doubted the princess, but that he wanted the fairy to tell him more. She was too old a fairy, however, to be caught so easily.

"Of all people, fairies must not tell secrets. Besides, she's a princess."

"Well, I'll tell *you* a secret. I'm a prince."

"I know that."

"How do you know it?"

"By the curl of the third eyelash on your left eyelid."

"Which corner do you count from?"

"That's a secret."

"Another secret? Well, at least, if I am a prince, there can be no harm in telling me about a princess."

"It's just princes I can't tell."

"There ain't any more of them—are there?" said the prince.

"What! you don't think you're the only prince in the world, do you?"

"Oh, dear, no! not at all. But I know there's one too many just at present, except the princess—"

"Yes, yes, that's it," said the fairy.

"What's *it*?" asked the prince.

But he could get nothing more out of the fairy, and had to go to bed unanswered, which was something of a trial.

Now wicked fairies will not be bound by the laws which the good fairies obey, and this always seems to give the bad the advantage over the good, for they use means to gain their ends which the others will not. But it is all of no consequence, for what they do never succeeds; nay, in the end it brings about the very thing they are trying to prevent. So you see that somehow, for all their cleverness, wicked fairies are dreadfully stupid, for, although from the beginning of the world they have really helped instead of thwarting the good fairies, not one of them is a bit the wiser for it. She will try the bad thing just as they all did before her; and succeed no better of course.

The prince had so far stolen a march upon the swamp-fairy that she did not know he was in the neighbourhood until after he had seen the princess those three times. When she knew it, she consoled herself by thinking that the princess must be far too proud and too modest for any young man to venture even to speak to her before he had seen her six times at least. But there was even less danger than the wicked fairy thought; for, however much the princess might desire to be set free, she was dreadfully afraid of the wrong prince. Now, however, the fairy was going to do all she could.

She so contrived it by her deceitful spells, that the next night the prince could not by any endeavour find his way to the glade. It would take me too long to tell her tricks. They would be amusing to us, who know that they could not do any harm, but they were something other than amusing to the poor prince. He wandered about the forest till daylight, and then fell fast asleep. The same thing occurred for seven following days, during which neither could he find the good fairy's cottage. After the third quarter of the moon, however, the bad fairy thought she might be at ease about the affair for a fortnight at least, for there was no chance of the prince wishing to kiss the princess during that period. So the first day of the fourth quarter he did find the cottage, and the next day he found the glade. For nearly another week he haunted it. But the princess never came. I have little doubt she was on the farther edge of it some part of every night, but at this period she always wore black, and, there being little or no light, the prince never saw her. Nor would he have known her if he had seen her. How could he have taken the worn decrepit creature she was now, for the glorious Princess Daylight?

At last, one night when there was no moon at all, he ventured near the house. There he heard voices talking, although it was past midnight; for her women were in considerable uneasiness, because the one whose turn it was to watch her had fallen asleep, and had not seen which way she went, and this was a night when she would probably wander very far, describing a circle which did not touch the open glade at all, but stretched away from the back of the house, deep into that side of the forest—a part of which the prince knew nothing. When he understood from what they said that she had disappeared, and that she must

have gone somewhere in the said direction, he plunged
at once into the wood to see if he could find her. For
hours he roamed with nothing to guide him but the
vague notion of a circle which on one side bordered
on the house, for so much had he picked up from the
talk he had overheard.

It was getting towards the dawn, but as yet there
was no streak of light in the sky, when he came to a
great birch-tree, and sat down weary at the foot of it.
While he sat—very miserable, you may be sure—full
of fear for the princess, and wondering how her attendants could take it so quietly, he bethought himself that it would not be a bad plan to light a fire,
which, if she were anywhere near, would attract her.
This he managed with a tinder-box, which the good
fairy had given him. It was just beginning to blaze
up, when he heard a moan, which seemed to come
from the other side of the tree. He sprung to his feet,
but his heart throbbed so that he had to lean for a
moment against the tree before he could move. When
he got round, there lay a human form in a little dark
heap on the earth. There was light enough from his
fire to show that it was not the princess. He lifted it
in his arms, hardly heavier than a child, and carried
it to the flame. The countenance was that of an old
woman, but it had a fearfully strange look. A black
hood concealed her hair, and her eyes were closed.
He laid her down as comfortably as he could, chafed
her hands, put a little cordial from a bottle, also the
gift of the fairy, into her mouth; took off his coat and
wrapped it about her, and in short did the best he
could. In a little while she opened her eyes and looked
at him—so pitifully! The tears rose and flowed down
her gray wrinkled cheeks, but she said never a word.
She closed her eyes again, but the tears kept on flowing, and her whole appearance was so utterly pitiful
that the prince was very near crying too. He begged

her to tell him what was the matter, promising to do all he could to help her; but still she did not speak. He thought she was dying, and took her in his arms again to carry her to the princess's house, where he thought the good-natured cook might be able to do something for her. When he lifted her, the tears flowed yet faster, and she gave such a sad moan that it went to his very heart.

"Mother, mother!" he said—"Poor mother!" and kissed her on the withered lips.

She started; and what eyes they were that opened upon him! But he did not see them, for it was still very dark, and he had enough to do to make his way through the trees towards the house.

Just as he approached the door, feeling more tired than he could have imagined possible—she was such a little thin old thing—she began to move, and became so restless that, unable to carry her a moment longer, he thought to lay her on the grass. But she stood upright on her feet. Her hood had dropped, and her hair fell about her. The first gleam of the morning was caught on her face: that face was bright as the never-ageing Dawn, and her eyes were lovely as the sky of darkest blue. The prince recoiled in over-mastering wonder. It was Daylight herself whom he had brought from the forest! He fell at her feet, nor dared look up until she laid her hand upon his head. He rose then.

"You kissed me when I was an old woman: there! I kiss you when I am a young princess," murmured Daylight.—"Is that the sun coming?"

CROSS PURPOSES

I

ONCE upon a time, the Queen of Fairyland, finding her own subjects far too well-behaved to be amusing, took a sudden longing to have a mortal or two at her Court. So, after looking about her for some time, she fixed upon two to bring to Fairyland.

But how were they to be brought?

"Please your majesty," said at last the daughter of the prime minister, "I will bring the girl,"

The speaker, whose name was Peaseblossom, after her great-great-grandmother, looked so graceful, and hung her head so apologetically, that the Queen said at once,—

"How will you manage it, Peaseblossom?"

"I will open the road before her, and close it behind her."

"I have heard that you have pretty ways of doing things; so you may try."

The court happened to be held in an open forest glade of smooth turf, upon which there was just one mole-heap. As soon as the Queen had given her permission to Peaseblossom, up through the mole-heap came the head of a goblin, which cried out,—

"Please your majesty, I will bring the boy."

"You!" exclaimed the Queen. "How will you do it?"

The goblin began to wriggle himself out of the earth,

Reprinted from *Dealings with Fairies* (1867).

Up through the Mole-heap
came the head of a goblin, Toadstool.

as if he had been a snake, and the whole world his skin, till the court was convulsed with laughter. As soon as he got free, he began to roll over and over, in every possible manner, rotatory and cylindrical, all at once, until he reached the wood. The courtiers followed, holding their sides, so that the Queen was left sitting upon her throne in solitary state. When they reached the wood, the goblin, whose name was Toadstool, was nowhere to be seen. While they were looking for him, out popped his head from the mole-heap again, with the words,—

"So, your majesty."

"You have taken your own time to answer," said the Queen, laughing.

"And my own way too, eh! your majesty?" rejoined Toadstool, grinning.

"No doubt. Well, you may try."

And the goblin, making as much of a bow as he could with only half his neck above-ground, disappeared under it.

II

NO mortal, or fairy either, can tell where Fairyland begins and where it ends. But somewhere on the border of Fairyland there was a nice country village, in which lived some nice country people.

Alice was the daughter of the squire, a pretty, good-natured girl, whom her friends called fairylike, and others called silly.—One rosy summer evening, when the wall opposite her window was flaked all over with rosiness, she threw herself on her bed, and lay gazing at the wall. The rose-colour sank through her eyes and eyed her brain, and she began to feel as if she were reading a story-book. She thought she was looking at a western sea, with the waves all red with sunset. But when the colour died out, Alice gave a sigh to see how commonplace the wall grew. "I wish it was always sunset!" she said, half aloud. "I don't like gray things."

"I will take you where the sun is always setting, if you like, Alice," said a sweet, tiny voice near her. She looked down on the coverlet of the bed, and there, looking up at her, stood a lovely little creature. It seemed quite natural that the little lady should be there; for many things we never could believe, have only to happen, and then there is nothing strange about them. She was dressed in white, with a cloak of sunset-red—the colours of the sweetest of sweet-peas. On her head was a crown of twisted tendrils, with a little gold beetle in front.

"Are you a fairy?" said Alice.

"Yes. Will you go with me to the sunset?"

"Yes, I will,"

When Alice proceeded to rise, she found that she was no bigger than the fairy; and when she stood up on the counterpane, the bed looked like a great hall with a painted ceiling. As she walked towards Pease-blossom, she stumbled several times over the tufts that made the pattern. But the fairy took her by the hand and led her towards the foot of the bed. Long before they reached it, however, Alice saw that the fairy was a tall, slender lady, and that she herself was quite her own size. What she had taken for tufts on the counterpane were really bushes of furze, and broom, and heather, on the side of a slope.

"Where are we?" asked Alice.

"Going on," answered the fairy.

Alice, not liking the reply, said,—

"I want to go home."

"Good-bye, then," answered the fairy.

Alice looked round. A wide, hilly country lay all about them. She could not even tell from what quarter they had come.

"I must go with you, I see," she said.

Before they reached the bottom, they were walking over the loveliest meadow-grass. A little stream went cantering down beside them, without channel or bank, sometimes running between the blades, sometimes sweeping the grass all one way under it. And it made a great babbling for such a little stream and such a smooth course.

Gradually the slope grew gentler, and the stream flowed more softly and spread out wider. At length they came to a wood of long, straight poplars, growing out of the water, for the stream ran into the wood, and there stretched out into a lake. Alice thought they could go no farther; but Peaseblossom led her straight on, and they walked through.

It was now dark; but everything under the water gave out a pale, quiet light. There were deep pools here and there, but there was no mud, or frogs, or water-lizards, or eels. All the bottom was pure, lovely grass, brilliantly green. Down the banks of the pools she saw, all under water, primroses and violets and pimpernels. Any flower she wished to see she had only to look for, and she was sure to find it. When a pool came in their way, the fairy swam, and Alice swam by her; and when they got out they were quite dry, though the water was as delightfully wet as water should be. Besides the trees, tall, splendid lilies grew out of it, and hollyhocks and irises and sword-plants, and many other long-stemmed flowers. From every leaf and petal of these, from every branch-tip and tendril, dropped bright water. It gathered slowly at each point, but the points were so many that there was a constant musical plashing of diamond rain upon the still surface of the lake. As they went on, the moon rose and threw a pale mist of light over the whole, and the diamond drops turned to half-liquid pearls, and round every tree-top was a halo of moonlight, and the water went to sleep, and the flowers began to dream.

"Look," said the fairy; "those lilies are just dreaming themselves into a child's sleep. I can see them smiling. This is the place out of which go the things that appear to children every night."

"Is this dreamland, then?" asked Alice.

"If you like," answered the fairy.

"How far am I from home?"

"The farther you go, the nearer home you are."

Then the fairy lady gathered a bundle of poppies and gave it to Alice. The next deep pool that they came to, she told her to throw it in. Alice did so, and following it, laid her head upon it. That moment she began to sink. Down and down she went, till at last she felt herself lying on the long, thick grass at the bottom of the pool, with the poppies under her head and the clear water high over it. Up through it she saw the moon, whose bright face looked sleepy too, disturbed only by the little ripples of the rain from the tall flowers on the edges of the pool.

She fell fast asleep, and all night dreamed about home.

III

RICHARD—which is name enough for a fairy story—was the son of a widow in Alice's village. He was so poor that he did not find himself generally welcome; so he hardly went anywhere, but read books at home, and waited upon his mother. His manners, therefore, were shy, and sufficiently awkward to give an unfavourable impression to those who looked at outsides. Alice would have despised him; but he never came near enough for that.

Now Richard had been saving up his few pence in order to buy an umbrella for his mother; for the winter would come, and the one she had was almost torn to ribands. One bright summer evening, when he thought umbrellas must be cheap, he was walking across the market-place to buy one; there, in the middle of it, stood an odd-looking little man, actually selling umbrellas. Here was a chance for him! When he drew nearer, he found that the little man, while vaunting his umbrellas to the skies, was asking such absurdly small prices for them, that no one would venture to buy one. He had opened and laid them all out in full stretch on the market-place—about five-and-twenty of them, stick downwards, like little tents—and he stood beside, haranguing the people. But he would not allow one of the crowd to touch his umbrellas. As soon as his eye fell upon Richard, he changed his tone, and said, "Well, as nobody seems inclined to buy, I think, my dear umbrellas, we had better be going home." Whereupon the umbrellas got up, with some difficulty, and began hobbling away. The people stared at each other with open mouths, for they saw that what they had taken for a lot of umbrellas, was in reality a flock of black geese. A great turkey-cock went gobbling behind them, driving them all down a lane towards the forest. Richard thought with himself, "There is more in this than I can account for. But an umbrella that could lay eggs would be a very jolly umbrella." So by the time the people were beginning to laugh at each other, Richard was halfway down the lane at the heels of the geese. There he stopped and caught one of them, but instead of a goose he had a huge hedgehog in his hands, which he dropped in dismay; whereupon it waddled away a goose as before, and the whole of them began cackling and hissing in a way that he could not mistake. For the turkey cock, he gobbled and gabbled and choked himself and got right again in the most ridiculous manner. In fact, he seemed sometimes to

forget that he was a turkey, and laughed like a fool.
All at once, with a simultaneous long-necked hiss,
they flew into the wood, and the turkey after them.
But Richard soon got up with them again, and found
them all hanging by their feet from the trees, in two
rows, one on each side of the path, while the turkey
was walking on. Him Richard followed; but the moment he reached the middle of the suspended geese,
from every side arose the most frightful hisses, and
their necks grew longer and longer, till there were
nearly thirty broad bills close to his head, blowing in
his face, in his ears, and at the back of his neck. But
the turkey, looking round and seeing what was going
on, turned and walked back. When he reached the
place, he looked up at the first and gobbled at him in
the wildest manner. That goose grew silent and
dropped from the tree. Then he went to the next, and
the next, and so on, till he had gobbled them all off
the trees, one after another. But when Richard expected to see them go after the turkey, there was
nothing there but a flock of huge mushrooms and
puff-balls.

"I have had enough of this," thought Richard. "I
will go home again."

"Go home, Richard," said a voice close to him.

Looking down, he saw, instead of the turkey, the
most comical-looking little man he had ever seen.

"Go home, Master Richard," repeated he, grinning.

"Not for your bidding," answered Richard.

"Come on then, Master Richard."

"Nor that either, without a good reason."

"I will give you *such* an umbrella for your mother."

"I don't take presents from strangers."

"Bless you, I'm no stranger here! Oh no! not at
all." And he set off in the manner usual with him,
rolling every way at once.

Richard could not help laughing and following. At

length Toadstool plumped into a great hole full of water. "Served him right!" thought Richard. "Served him right!" bawled the goblin, crawling out again, and shaking the water from him like a spaniel. "This is the very place I wanted, only I rolled too fast." However, he went on rolling again faster than before, though it was now up hill, till he came to the top of a considerable height, on which grew a number of palm trees.

"Have you a knife, Richard?" said the goblin, stopping all at once, as if he had been walking quietly along, just like other people.

Richard pulled out a pocket-knife and gave it to the creature, who instantly cut a deep gash in one of the trees. Then he bounded to another and did the same, and so on, till he had gashed them all. Richard, following him, saw that a little stream, clearer than the clearest water, began to flow from each, increasing in size the longer it flowed. Before he had reached the last there was quite a tinkling and rustling of little rills that run down the stems of the palms. This grew and grew, till Richard saw that a full rivulet was flowing down the side of the hill.

"Here is your knife, Richard," said the goblin; but by the time he had put it in his pocket, the rivulet had grown to a small torrent.

"Now, Richard, come along," said Toadstool, and threw himself into the torrent.

"I would rather have a boat," returned Richard.

"Oh, you stupid!" cried Toadstool, crawling up the side of the hill, down which the stream had already carried him some distance.

With every contortion that labour and difficulty could suggest, yet with incredible rapidity, he crawled to the very top of one of the trees, and tore down a huge leaf, which he threw on the ground, and himself after it, rebounding like a ball. He then laid the leaf

on the water, held it by the stem, and told Richard to
get upon it. He did so. It went down deep in the
middle with his weight. Toadstool let it go, and it shot
down the stream like an arrow. Thus began the
strangest and most delightful voyage. The stream
rushed careering and curveting down the hill-side,
bright as a diamond, and soon reached a meadow
plain. The goblin rolled alongside of the boat like a
bundle of weeds; but Richard rode in triumph through
the low grassy country upon the back of his watery
steed. It went straight as an arrow, and, strange to
tell, was heaped up on the ground, like a ridge of
water or a wave, only rushing on endways. It needed
no channel, and turned aside for no opposition. It
flowed over everything that crossed its path, like a
great serpent of water, with folds fitting into all the
ups and downs of the way. If a wall came in its course
it flowed against it, heaping itself up on itself till it
reached the top, whence it plunged to the foot on the
other side, and flowed on. Soon he found that it was
running gently up a grassy hill. The waves kept curl-
ing back as if the wind blew them, or as if they could
hardly keep from running down again. But still the
stream mounted and flowed, and the waves with it.
It found it difficult, but it could do it. When they
reached the top, it bore them across a heathy country, rolling over purple heather, and blue harebells,
and delicate ferns, and tall foxgloves crowded with
bells purple and white. All the time, the palm-leaf
curled its edges away from the water, and made a
delightful boat for Richard, while Toadstool tumbled
along in the stream like a porpoise. At length the
water began to run very fast, and went faster and
faster, till suddenly it plunged them into a deep lake,
with a great splash, and stopped there. Toadstool went
out of sight, and came up gasping and grinning, while
Richard's boat tossed and heaved like a vessel in a

storm at sea; but not a drop of water came in. Then
the goblin began to swim, and pushed and tugged the
boat along. But the lake was so still, and the motion
so pleasant, that Richard fell fast asleep.

IV

WHEN he woke, he found himself still afloat upon
the broad palm-leaf. He was alone in the middle
of a lake, with flowers and trees growing in and out
of it everywhere. The sun was just over the tree-tops.
A drip of water from the flowers greeted him with
music; the mists were dissolving away; and where
the sunlight fell on the lake the water was clear as
glass. Casting his eyes downward, he saw, just beneath him, far down at the bottom, Alice—drowned,
as he thought. He was in the act of plunging in, when
he saw her open her eyes, and at the same moment
begin to float up. He held out his hand, but she re-
pelled it with disdain; and swimming to a tree, sat
down on a low branch, wondering how ever the poor
widow's son could have found his way into Fairyland.
She did not like it. It was an invasion of privilege.

"How did you come here, young Richard?" she
asked, from six yards off.

"A goblin brought me."

"Ah, I thought so. A fairy brought me."

"Where is your fairy?"

"Here I am," said Peaseblossom, rising slowly to
the surface, just by the tree on which Alice was seated.

"Where is your goblin?" retorted Alice.

"Here I am," bawled Toadstool, rushing out of the
water like a salmon, and casting a sumersault in the
air before he fell in again with a tremendous splash.
His head rose again close beside Peaseblossom, who
being used to such creatures only laughed.

"Isn't he handsome?" he grinned.

"Yes, very. He wants polishing though."

"You could do that for yourself, you know. Shall we change?"

"I don't mind. You'll find her rather silly."

"That's nothing. The boy's too sensible for me."

He dived, and rose at Alice's feet. She shrieked with terror. The fairy floated away like a water-lily towards Richard. "What a lovely creature!" thought he, but hearing Alice shriek again, he said,

"Don't leave Alice, she's frightened at that queer creature.—I don't think there's any harm in him, though, Alice."

"Oh, no. He won't hurt her," said Peaseblossom. "I'm tired of her. He's going to take her to the court, and I will take you."

"I don't want to go."

"But you must. You can't go home again. You don't know the way."

"Richard! Richard!" cried Alice, in an agony.

Richard sprang from his boat, and was by her side in a moment.

"He pinched me," cried Alice.

Richard hit the goblin a terrible blow on the head; but it took no more effect upon him than if his head had been a round ball of India-rubber. He gave Richard a furious look, however, and bawling out, "You'll repent that, Dick!" vanished under the water.

"Come along, Richard, make haste; he will murder you," cried the fairy.

"It is all your fault," said Richard. "I won't leave Alice."

Then the fairy saw it was all over with her and Toadstool; for they can do nothing with mortals against their will. So she floated away across the water in Richard's boat, holding her robe for a sail, and vanished, leaving the two alone in the lake.

"You have driven away my fairy!" cried Alice. "I

shall never get home now. It is all your fault, you naughty young man."

"I drove away the goblin," remonstrated Richard.

"Will you please to sit on the other side of the tree. I wonder what my papa would say if he saw me talking to you!"

"Will you come to the next tree, Alice?" said Richard, after a pause.

Alice, who had been crying all the time that Richard was thinking, said, "I won't." Richard, therefore, plunged into the water without her, and swam for the tree. Before he had got half-way, however, he heard Alice crying, "Richard! Richard!" This was just what he wanted. So he turned back, and Alice threw herself into the water. With Richard's help she swam pretty well, and they reached the tree. "Now for the next!" said Richard; and they swam to the next, and then to the third. Every tree they reached was larger than the last, and every tree before them was larger still. So they swam from tree to tree, till they came to one that was so large that they could not see round it. What was to be done? Clearly, to climb this tree. It was a dreadful prospect for Alice, but Richard proceeded to climb; and by putting her feet where he put his, and now and then getting hold of his ankle, she managed to make her way up. There were a great many stumps where branches had withered off, and the bark was nearly as rough as a hill-side, so there was plenty of foothold for them. When they had climbed a long time, and were getting very tired indeed, Alice cried out, "Richard, I shall drop—I shall. Why did you come this way?" And she began once more to cry. But at that moment Richard caught hold of a branch above his head, and reaching down his other hand got hold of Alice, and held her till she had recovered a little. In a few moments they reached the fork of the tree, and there they sat and rested. "This is capital!" said Richard, cheerily.

"What is?" asked Alice, sulkily.

"Why, we have room to rest, and there's no hurry for a minute or two. I'm tired."

"You selfish creature!" said Alice. "If you are tired, what must I be?"

"Tired too," answered Richard. "But we've got on bravely. And look! what's that?"

By this time the day was gone, and the night so near, that in the shadows of the tree all was dusky and dim. But there was still light enough to discover that in a niche of the tree sat a huge horned owl, with green spectacles on his beak, and a book in one foot. He took no heed of the intruders, but kept muttering to himself. And what do you think the owl was saying? I will tell you. He was talking about the book that he held upside down in his foot.

"Stupid book this-s-s-s! Nothing in it at all! Everything upside down! Stupid ass-s-s-s! Says owls can't read! *I* can read backwards!"

"I think that is the goblin again," said Richard, in a whisper. "However, if you ask a plain question, he

144

must give you a plain answer, for they are not allowed to tell downright lies in Fairyland."

"Don't ask him, Richard; you know you gave him a dreadful blow."

"I gave him what he deserved, and he owes me the same.—Hallo! which is the way out?"

He wouldn't say *if you please*, because then it would not have been a plain question.

"Down stairs," hissed the owl, without ever lifting his eyes from the book, which all the time he read upside down, so learned was he.

"On your honour, as a respectable old owl?" asked Richard.

"No," hissed the owl; and Richard was almost sure that he was not really an owl. So he stood staring at him for a few moments, when all at once, without lifting his eyes from the book, the owl said, "I will sing a song," and began:—

"Nobody knows the world but me.
When they're all in bed, I sit up to see.
I'm a better student than students all,
For I never read till the darkness fall;
And I never read without my glasses,
And that is how my wisdom passes.
Howlowlwhoolhoolwoolool.

"I can see the wind. Now who can do that?
I see the dreams that he has in his hat;
I see him snorting them out as he goes —
Out at his stupid old trumpet-nose.
Ten thousand things that you couldn't think
I write them down with pen and ink.
Howlowlwhooloolwhitit that's wit.

"You may call it learning — 'tis mother-wit.
No one else sees the lady-moon sit
On the sea, her nest, all night, but the owl,
Hatching the boats and the long-legged fowl.
When the oysters gape to sing by rote,
She crams a pearl down each stupid throat.
Howlowlwhitit that's wit, there's a fowl!"

And so singing, he threw the book in Richard's face, spread out his great, silent, soft wings, and sped away into the depths of the tree. When the book struck Richard, he found that it was only a lump of wet moss.

While talking to the owl he had spied a hollow behind one of the branches. Judging this to be the way the owl meant, he went to see, and found a rude, ill-defined staircase going down into the very heart of the trunk. But so large was the tree that this could not have hurt it in the least. Down this stair, then, Richard scrambled as best he could, followed by Alice—not of her own will, she gave him clearly to understand, but because she could do no better. Down, down they went, slipping and falling sometimes, but never very far, because the stair went round and round. It caught Richard when he slipped, and he caught Alice when she did. They had begun to fear that there was no end to the stair, it went round and round so steadily, when, creeping through a crack, they found themselves in a great hall, supported by thousands of pillars of gray stone. Where the little light came from they could not tell. This hall they began to cross in a straight line, hoping to reach one side, and intending to walk along it till they came to some opening. They kept straight by going from pillar to pillar, as they had done before by the trees. Any honest plan will do in Fairyland, if you only stick to it. And no plan will do if you do not stick to it.

It was very silent, and Alice disliked the silence more than the dimness,—so much, indeed, that she longed to hear Richard's voice. But she had always been so cross to him when he had spoken, that he thought it better to let her speak first; and she was too proud to do that. She would not even let him walk alongside of her, but always went slower when he wanted to wait for her; so that at last he strode on alone. And Alice followed. But by degrees the horror of silence grew upon her, and she felt at last as if there was no one in the universe but herself. The hall went on widening around her; their footsteps made no noise; the silence grew so intense that it seemed on the point of taking shape. At last she could bear it no longer. She ran after Richard, got up with him, and laid hold of his arm.

He had been thinking for some time what an obstinate, disagreeable girl Alice was, and wishing he had her safe home to be rid of her, when, feeling a hand, and looking round, he saw that it was the disagreeable girl. She soon began to be companionable after a fashion, for she began to think, putting everything together, that Richard must have been several times in Fairyland before now. "It is very strange," she said to herself; "for he is quite a poor boy, I am sure of that. His arms stick out beyond his jacket like the ribs of his mother's umbrella. And to think of me wandering about Fairyland with *him!*"

The moment she touched his arm, they saw an arch of blackness before them. They had walked straight to a door—not a very inviting one, for it opened upon an utterly dark passage. Where there was only one door, however, there was no difficulty about choosing. Richard walked straight through it; and from the greater fear of being left behind, Alice

147

faced the lesser fear of going on. In a moment they were in total darkness. Alice clung to Richard's arm, and murmured, almost against her will, "Dear Richard!" It was strange that fear should speak like love; but it was in Fairyland. It was strange, too, that as soon as she spoke thus, Richard should fall in love with her all at once. But what was more curious still was, that, at the same moment, Richard saw her face. In spite of her fear, which had made her pale, she looked very lovely.

"Dear Alice!" said Richard, "How pale you look!"

"How can you tell that, Richard, when all is as black as pitch?"

"I can see your face. It gives out light. Now I see your hands. Now I can see your feet. Yes, I can see every spot where you are going to—No, don't put your foot there. There is an ugly toad just there."

The fact was, that the moment he began to love Alice, his eyes began to send forth light. What he thought came from Alice's face, really came from his eyes. All about her and her path he could see, and every minute saw better; but to his own path he was blind. He could not see his hand when he held it straight before his face, so dark was it. But he could see Alice, and that was better than seeing the way— ever so much.

At length Alice too began to see a face dawning through the darkness. It was Richard's face: but it was far handsomer than when she saw it last. Her eyes had begun to give light too. And she said to herself—"Can it be that I love the poor widow's son?— I suppose that must be it," she answered herself, with a smile; for she was not disgusted with herself at all. Richard saw the smile, and was glad. Her paleness had gone, and a sweet rosiness had taken its place. And now she saw Richard's path as he saw hers, and between the two sights they got on well.

They were now walking on a path betwixt two deep waters, which never moved, shining as black as ebony where the eyelight fell. But they saw ere long that this path kept growing narrower and narrower. At last, to Alice's dismay, the black waters met in front of them.

"What is to be done now, Richard?" she said.

When they fixed their eyes on the water before them, they saw that it was swarming with lizards, and frogs, and black snakes, and all kinds of strange and ugly creatures, especially some that had neither heads, nor tails, nor legs, nor fins, nor feelers, being, in fact, only living lumps. These kept jumping out and in, and sprawling upon the path. Richard thought for a few moments before replying to Alice's question, as, indeed, well he might. But he came to the conclusion that the path could not have gone on for the sake of stopping there; and that it must be a kind of finger that pointed on where it was not allowed to go itself. So he caught up Alice in his strong arms, and jumped into the middle of the horrid swarm. And just as minnows vanish if you throw anything amongst them, just so these wretched creatures vanished, right and left and every way.

He found the water broader than he had expected; and before he got over, he found Alice heavier than he could have believed; but upon a firm, rocky bottom, Richard waded through in safety. When he reached the other side, he found that the bank was a lofty, smooth, perpendicular rock, with some rough steps cut in it. By-and-by the steps led them right into the rock, and they were in a narrow passage once more, but, this time, leading up. It wound round and round, like the thread of a great screw. At last, Richard knocked his head against something, and could go no farther. The place was close and hot. He put up his hands, and pushed what felt like a warm stone: it moved a little.

"Go down, you brutes!" growled a voice above, quivering with anger. "You'll upset my pot and my cat, and my temper, too, if you push that way. Go down!"

Richard knocked very gently, and said: "Please let us out."

"O yes, I dare say! Very fine and soft-spoken! Go down, you goblin brutes! I've had enough of you. I'll scald the hair off your ugly heads if you do that again. Go down, I say!"

Seeing fair speech was of no avail, Richard told Alice to go down a little, out of the way; and, setting his shoulders to one end of the stone, heaved it up; whereupon down came the other end, with a pot, and a fire, and a cat which had been asleep beside it. She frightened Alice dreadfully as she rushed past her, showing nothing but her green lamping eyes.

Richard, peeping up, found that he had turned a hearthstone upside down. On the edge of the hole stood a little crooked old man, brandishing a mop-stick in a tremendous rage, and hesitating only where to strike him. But Richard put him out of his difficulty by springing up and taking the stick from him. Then, having lifted Alice out, he returned it with a bow, and, heedless of the maledictions of the old man, proceeded to get the stone and the pot up again. For puss, she got out of herself.

Then the old man became a little more friendly, and said: "I beg your pardon, I thought you were goblins. They never will let me alone. But you must allow, it was rather an unusual way of paying a morning call." And the creature bowed conciliatingly.

"It was, indeed," answered Richard. "I wish you had turned the door to us instead of the hearthstone."

For he did not trust the old man. "But," he added, "I hope you will forgive us."

"Oh, certainly, certainly, my dear young people. Use your freedom. But such young people have no business to be out alone. It is against the rules."

"But what is one to do—I mean two to do—when they can't help it?"

"Yes, yes, of course; but now, you know, I must take charge of you. So you sit there, young gentleman; and you sit there, young lady."

He put a chair for one at one side of the hearth, and for the other at the other side, and then drew his chair between them. The cat got upon his hump, and then set up her own. So here was a wall that would let through no moonshine. But although both Richard and Alice were very much amused, they did not like to be parted in this peremptory manner. Still they thought it better not to anger the old man any more— in his own house, too.

But he had been once angered, and that was once too often, for he had made it a rule never to forgive without taking it out in humiliation.

It was so disagreeable to have him sitting there between them, that they felt as if they were far asunder. In order to get the better of the fancy, they wanted to hold each other's hand behind the dwarf's back. But the moment their hands began to approach, the back of the cat began to grow long, and its hump to grow high; and, in a moment more, Richard found himself crawling wearily up a steep hill, whose ridge rose against the stars, while a cold wind blew drearily over it. Not a habitation was in sight; and Alice had vanished from his eyes. He felt, however, that she must be somewhere on the other side, and so climbed and climbed, to get over the brow of the hill, and down to where he thought she must be. But the longer he climbed, the farther off the top of the hill seemed;

151

till at last he sank quite exhausted, and—must I confess it?—very nearly began to cry. To think of being
separated from Alice, all at once, and in such a disagreeable way! But he fell a-thinking instead, and soon
said to himself: "This must be some trick of that
wretched old man. Either this mountain is a cat or
it is not. If it is a mountain, this won't hurt it; if it is
a cat, I hope it will." With that, he pulled out his
pocket-knife, and feeling for a soft place, drove it at
one blow up to the handle in the side of the mountain.

A terrific shriek was the first result; and the second, that Alice and he sat looking at each other across
the old man's hump, from which the cat-a-mountain
had vanished. Their host sat staring at the blank fire-
place, without ever turning round, pretending to know
nothing of what had taken place.

"Come along, Alice," said Richard, rising. "This
won't do. We won't stop here."

Alice rose at once, and put her hand in his. They
walked towards the door. The old man took no notice
of them. The moon was shining brightly through the
window; but instead of stepping out into the moonlight when they opened the door, they stepped into
a great beautiful hall, through the high gothic windows of which the same moon was shining. Out of
this hall they could find no way, except by a staircase
of stone which led upwards. They ascended it together. At the top Alice let go Richard's hand to peep
into a little room, which looked all the colours of the
rainbow, just like the inside of a diamond. Richard
went a step or two along a corridor, but finding she
had left him, turned and looked into the chamber. He
could see her nowhere. The room was full of doors;
and she must have mistaken the door. He heard her
voice calling him, and hurried in the direction of the
sound. But he could see nothing of her. "More tricks,"
he said to himself. "It is of no use to stab this one.

I must wait till I see what can be done." Still he heard Alice calling him, and still he followed, as well as he could. At length he came to a doorway, open to the air, through which the moonlight fell. But when he reached it, he found that it was high up in the side of a tower, the wall of which went straight down from his feet, without stair or descent of any kind. Again he heard Alice call him, and lifting his eyes, saw her, across a wide castle-court, standing at another door just like the one he was at, with the moon shining full upon her.

"All right, Alice!" he cried. "Can you hear me?"

"Yes," answered she.

"Then listen. This is all a trick. It is all a lie of that old wretch in the kitchen. Just reach out your hand, Alice dear."

Alice did as Richard asked her; and, although they saw each other many yards off across the court, their hands met.

"There! I thought so!" exclaimed Richard, triumphantly. "Now, Alice, I don't believe it is more than a foot or two down to the court below, though it looks like a hundred feet. Keep fast hold of my hand, and jump when I count three." But Alice drew her hand from him in sudden dismay; whereupon Richard said, "Well, I will try first," and jumped. The same moment, his cheery laugh came to Alice's ears, and she saw him standing safe on the ground, far below.

"Jump, dear Alice, and I will catch you," said he.

"I can't; I am afraid," answered she.

"The old man is somewhere near you. You had better jump," said Richard.

Alice jumped from the wall in terror, and only fell a foot or two into Richard's arms. The moment she touched the ground, they found themselves outside the door of a little cottage which they knew very well, for it was only just within the wood that bordered on their village. Hand in hand they ran home as fast as they could. When they reached a little gate that led into her father's grounds, Richard bade Alice good-bye. The tears came in her eyes. Richard and she seemed to have grown quite man and woman in Fairyland, and they did not want to part now. But they felt that they must. So Alice ran in the back way, and reached her own room before any one had missed her. Indeed, the last of the red had not quite faded from the west.

As Richard crossed the market-place on his way home, he saw an umbrella-man just selling the last of his umbrellas. He thought the man gave him a queer look as he passed, and felt very much inclined to punch his head. But remembering how useless it had been to punch the goblin's head, he thought it better not.

In reward of their courage, the Fairy Queen sent them permission to visit Fairyland as often as they pleased; and no goblin or fairy was allowed to interfere with them.

For Peaseblossom and Toadstool, they were both banished from court, and compelled to live together, for seven years, in an old tree that had just one green leaf upon it.

Toadstool did not mind it much, but Peaseblossom did.

THE CASTLE=A PARABLE

O N the top of a high cliff, forming part of the base of a great mountain, stood a lofty castle. When or how it was built, no man knew; nor could any one pretend to understand its architecture. Every one who looked upon it felt that it was lordly and noble; and where one part seemed not to agree with another, the wise and modest dared not to call them incongruous, but presumed that the whole might be constructed on some higher principle of architecture than they yet understood. What helped them to this conclusion was, that no one had ever seen the whole of the edifice; that, even of the portion best known, some part or other was always wrapt in thick folds of mist from the mountain; and that, when the sun shone upon this mist, the parts of the building that appeared through the vaporous veil, were strangely glorified in their indistinctness, so that they seemed to belong to some aerial abode in the land of the sunset; and the beholders could hardly tell whether they had ever seen them before, or whether they were now for the first time partially revealed.

Nor, although it was inhabited, could certain information be procured as to its internal construction. Those who dwelt in it often discovered rooms they had never entered before; yea, once or twice, whole suites of apartments, of which only dim legends had

Reprinted from *Adela Cathcart* (1864).

*On the top of a high cliff stood a lofty castle
wrapped in thick folds of mist.*

been handed down from former times. Some of them expected to find, one day, secret places, filled with treasures of wondrous jewels, amongst which they hoped to light upon Solomon's ring, which had for ages disappeared from the earth, but which had controlled the spirits, and the possession of which made a man simply what a man should be, the king of the world. Now and then, a narrow, winding stair, hitherto untrodden, would bring them forth on a new turret, whence new prospects of the circumjacent country were spread out before them. How many more of these there might be, or how much loftier, no one could tell. Nor could the foundations of the castle in the rock on which it was built be determined with the smallest approach to precision. Those of the family who had given themselves to exploring in that direction, found such a labyrinth of vaults and passages, and endless successions of down-going stairs, out of one underground space into a yet lower, that they came to the conclusion that at least the whole mountain was perforated and honeycombed in this fashion. They had a dim consciousness, too, of the presence, in those awful regions, of beings whom they could not comprehend. Once, they came upon the brink of a great black gulf, in which the eye could see nothing but darkness: they recoiled in horror; for the conviction flashed upon them that that gulf went down into the very central spaces of the earth, of which they had hitherto been wandering only in the upper crust; nay, that the seething blackness before them had relations mysterious, and beyond human comprehension, with the far-off voids of space, into which the stars dare not enter.

At the foot of the cliff whereon the castle stood, lay a deep lake, inaccessible save by a few avenues, being surrounded on all sides with precipices, which made the water look very black, although it was as pure as the night-sky. From a door in the castle, which was not to be otherwise entered, a broad flight of steps, cut in the rock, went down to the lake, and disappeared below its surface. Some thought the steps went to the very bottom of the water.

Now in this castle there dwelt a large family of brothers and sisters. They had never seen their father or mother. The younger had been educated by the elder, and these by an unseen care and ministration, about the sources of which they had, somehow or other, troubled themselves very little, for what people are accustomed to, they regard as coming from no-body; as if help and progress and joy and love were the natural crops of Chaos or old Night. But Tradition said that one day—it was utterly uncertain *when*— their father would come, and leave them no more; for he was still alive, though where he lived nobody knew. In the meantime all the rest had to obey their eldest brother, and listen to his counsels.

But almost all the family was very fond of liberty, as they called it; and liked to run up and down, hither and thither, roving about, with neither law nor order, just as they pleased. So they could not endure their brother's tyranny, as they called it. At one time they said that he was only one of themselves, and there-fore they would not obey him; at another, that he was not like them, and could not understand them, and *therefore* they would not obey him. Yet, sometimes, when he came and looked them full in the face, they were terrified, and dared not disobey, for he was stately, and stern, and strong. Not one of them loved him heartily, except the eldest sister, who was very beautiful and silent, and whose eyes shone as if light lay somewhere deep behind them. Even she, al-though she loved him, thought him very hard some-times; for when he had once said a thing plainly, he could not be persuaded to think it over again. So even she forgot him sometimes, and went her own ways, and enjoyed herself without him. Most of them regarded him as a sort of watchman, whose business it was to keep them in order; and so they were indignant and disliked him. Yet they all had a secret feeling that they ought to be subject to him; and after any particular act of disregard, none of them could think, with any peace, of the old story about the return of their father to his house. But indeed they never thought much about it, or about their father at all; for how could those who cared so little for their brother, whom they saw every day, care for their father whom they had never seen?—One chief cause of complaint against him was, that he interfered with their favourite studies and pursuits; whereas he only sought to make them give up trifling with earnest things, and seek for truth, and not for amusement, from the many wonders around them. He did not want them to turn to other studies, or to eschew pleasures; but, in those studies, to seek the highest things most, and other things in proportion to their true worth and nobleness. This could not fail to be distasteful to those who did not care for what was higher than they. And so matters went on for a time. They thought they could do better without their brother; and their brother knew they could not do at all without him, and tried to fulfil the charge committed into his hands.

At length, one day, for the thought seemed to strike them simultaneously, they conferred together about giving a great entertainment in their grandest rooms to any of their neighbours who chose to come, or indeed to any inhabitants of the earth or air who would visit them. They were too proud to reflect that some company might defile even the dwellers in what was undoubtedly the finest palace on the face of the earth. But what made the thing worse, was, that the old tradition said that these rooms were to be kept entirely for the use of the owner of the castle. And, indeed, whenever they entered them, such was the effect of their loftiness and grandeur upon their minds, that they always thought of the old story, and could not help believing it. Nor would the brother permit them to forget it now; but, appearing suddenly amongst them, when they had no expectation of being interrupted by him, he rebuked them, both for the indiscriminate nature of their invitation, and for the intention of introducing any one, not to speak of some who would doubtless make their appearance on the evening in question, into the rooms kept sacred for the use of the unknown father. But by this time their talk with each other had so excited their expectations of enjoyment, which had previously been strong enough, that anger sprung up within them at the thought of being deprived of their hopes, and they looked each other in the eyes; and the look said: "We are many, and he is one—let us get rid of him, for he is always finding fault, and thwarting us in the most innocent pleasures;—as if we would wish to do any-thing wrong!" So without a word spoken, they rushed upon him; and although he was stronger than any of them, and struggled hard at first, yet they overcame him at last. Indeed some of them thought he yielded to their violence long before they had the mastery of him; and this very submission terrified the more tender-hearted among them. However, they bound him; carried him down many stairs, and, having re-membered an iron staple in the wall of a certain vault, with a thick rusty chain attached to it, they bore him thither, and made the chain fast around him. There they left him, shutting the great gnarring brazen door of the vault, as they departed for the upper regions of the castle.

Now all was in a tumult of preparation. Every one was talking of the coming festivity; but no one spoke

of the deed they had done. A sudden paleness overspread the face, now of one, and now of another; but
it passed away, and no one took any notice of it; they
only plied the task of the moment the more energet-
ically. Messengers were sent far and near, not to individuals or families, but publishing in all places of
concourse a general invitation to any who chose to
come on a certain day, and partake for certain suc-
ceeding days, of the hospitality of the dwellers in the
castle. Many were the preparations immediately begun for complying with the invitation. But the noblest
of their neighbours refused to appear; not from pride,
but because of the unsuitableness and carelessness
of such a mode. With some of them it was an old
condition in the tenure of their estates, that they
should go to no one's dwelling except visited in person, and expressly solicited. Others, knowing what
sorts of persons would be there, and that, from a
certain physical antipathy, they could scarcely breathe
in their company, made up their minds at once not
to go. Yet multitudes, many of them beautiful and
innocent as well as gay, resolved to appear.

Meanwhile the great rooms of the castle were got
in readiness—that is, they proceeded to deface them
with decorations; for there was a solemnity and state-
liness about them in their ordinary condition, which
was at once felt to be unsuitable for the light-hearted
company so soon to move about in them with the
self-same carelessness with which men walk abroad
within the great heavens and hills and clouds. One
day, while the workmen were busy, the eldest sister,
of whom I have already spoken, happened to enter,
she knew not why. Suddenly the great idea of the
mighty halls dawned upon her, and filled her soul.
The so-called decorations vanished from her view,
and she felt as if she stood in her father's presence.
She was at once elevated and humbled. As suddenly

161

the idea faded and fled, and she beheld but the gaudy festoons and draperies and paintings which disfigured the grandeur. She wept and sped away. Now it was too late to interfere, and things must take their course. She would have been but a Cassandra-prophetess to those who saw but the pleasure before them. She had not been present when her brother was imprisoned; and indeed for some days had been so wrapt in her own business, that she had taken but little heed of anything that was going on. But they all expected her to show herself when the company was gathered; and they had applied to her for advice at various times during their operations.

At length the expected hour arrived, and the company began to assemble. It was a warm summer evening. The dark lake reflected the rose-coloured clouds in the west, and through the flush rowed many gaily-painted boats, with various coloured flags, towards the massy rock on which the castle stood. The trees and flowers seemed already asleep, and breathing forth their sweet dream-breath. Laughter and low voices rose from the breast of the lake to the ears of the youths and maidens looking forth expectant from the lofty windows. They went down to the broad platform at the top of the stairs in front of the door to receive their visitors. By degrees the festivities of the evening commenced. The same smiles flew forth both at eyes and lips, darting like beams through the gathering crowd. Music, from unseen sources, now rolled in billows, now crept in ripples through the sea of air that filled the lofty rooms. And in the dancing halls, when hand took hand, and form and motion were moulded and swayed by the indwelling music, it governed not these alone, but, as the ruling spirit of the place, every new burst of music for a new dance swept before it a new and accordant odour, and dyed the flames that glowed in the lofty lamps with a new and accordant stain. The floors bent beneath the feet of the time-keeping dancers. But twice in the evening some of the inmates started, and the pallor occasionally common to the household overspread their faces, for they felt underneath them a counter-motion to the dance, as if the floor rose slightly to answer their feet. And all the time their brother lay below in the dungeon, like John the Baptist in the castle of Herod, when the lords and captains sat around, and the daughter of Herodias danced before them. Outside, all around the castle, brooded the dark night unheeded; for the clouds had come up from all sides, and were crowding together overhead. In the unfrequent pauses of the music, they might have heard, now and then, the gusty rush of a lonely wind, coming and going no one could know whence or whither, born and dying unexpected and unregarded.

But when the festivities were at their height, when the external and passing confidence which is produced between superficial natures by a common pleasure, was at the full, a sudden crash of thunder quelled the music, as the thunder quells the noise of the uplifted sea. The windows were driven in, and torrents of rain, carried in the folds of a rushing wind, poured into the halls. The lights were swept away; and the great rooms, now dark within, were darkened yet more by the dazzling shoots of flame from the vault of blackness overhead. Those that ventured to look out of the windows saw, in the blue brilliancy of the quick-following jets of lightning, the lake at the foot of the rock, ordinarily so still and so dark, lighted up, not on the surface only, but down to half its depth; so that, as it tossed in the wind, like a tortured sea of writhing flames, or incandescent half-molten serpents of brass, they could not tell whether a strong phosphorescence did not issue from the transparent body of the waters, as if earth and sky lightened together, one consenting source of flaming utterance.

Sad was the condition of the late plastic mass of living form that had flowed into shape at the will and law of the music. Broken into individuals, the common transfusing spirit withdrawn, they stood drenched, cold, and benumbed, with clinging garments; light, order, harmony, purpose departed, and chaos restored; the issuings of life turned back on their sources, chilly and dead. And in every heart reigned that falsest of despairing convictions, that this was the only reality, and that was but a dream. The eldest sister stood with clasped hands and down-bent head, shivering and speechless, as if waiting for something to follow. Nor did she wait long. A terrible flash and thunder-peal made the castle rock; and in the pausing silence that followed, her quick sense heard the rattling of a chain far off, deep down; and soon the sound of heavy footsteps, accompanied with the clanking of iron, reached her ear. She felt that her brother was at hand. Even in the darkness, and amidst the bellowing of another deep-bosomed cloud-monster, she knew that he had entered the room. A moment after, a continuous pulsation of angry blue light began, which, lasting for some moments, revealed him standing amidst them, gaunt, haggard, and motionless; his hair and beard untrimmed, his face ghastly, his eyes large and hollow. The light seemed to gather around him as a centre. Indeed some believed that it throbbed and radiated from his person, and not from the stormy heavens above them. The lightning had rent the wall of his prison, and released the iron staple of his chain, which he had wound about him like a girdle. In his hand he carried an iron fetter-bar, which he had found on the floor of the vault. More terrified at his aspect than at all the violence of the storm, the visitors, with many a shriek and cry, rushed out into the tempestuous night. By degrees, the storm died away. Its last flash revealed the forms of the brothers and sisters lying prostrate, with their faces on the floor, and that fearful shape standing motionless amidst them still.

Morning dawned, and there they lay, and there he stood. But at a word from him, they arose and went about their various duties, though listlessly enough. The eldest sister was the last to rise; and when she did, it was only by a terrible effort that she was able to reach her room, where she fell again on the floor. There she remained lying for days. The brother caused the doors of the great suite of rooms to be closed, leaving them just as they were, with all the childish adornment scattered about, and the rain still falling in through the shattered windows. "Thus let them lie," said he, "till the rain and frost have cleansed them of paint and drapery: no storm can hurt the pillars and arches of these halls."

The hours of this day went heavily. The storm was gone, but the rain was left; the passion had departed, but the tears remained behind. Dull and dark the low misty clouds brooded over the castle and the lake, and shut out all the neighbourhood. Even if they had climbed to the loftiest known turret, they would have found it swathed in a garment of clinging vapour, affording no refreshment to the eye, and no hope to the heart. There was one lofty tower that rose sheer a hundred feet above the rest, and from which the fog could have been seen lying in a grey mass beneath; but that tower they had not yet discovered, nor another close beside it, the top of which was never seen, nor could be, for the highest clouds of heaven clustered continually around it. The rain fell continuously, though not heavily, without; and within, too, there were clouds from which dropped the tears which are the rain of the spirit. All the good of life seemed for the time departed, and their souls lived but as leafless trees that had forgotten the joy of the summer, and whom no wind prophetic of spring had yet visited. They moved about mechanically, and had not strength enough left to wish to die.

The next day the clouds were higher, and a little wind blew through such loopholes in the turrets as the false improvements of the inmates had not yet filled with glass, shutting out, as the storm, so the serene visitings of the heavens. Throughout the day, the brother took various opportunities of addressing a gentle command, now to one and now to another of his family. It was obeyed in silence. The wind blew fresher through the loopholes and the shattered windows of the great rooms, and found its way, by unknown passages, to faces and eyes hot with weeping. It cooled and blessed them.—When the sun arose the next day, it was in a clear sky.

By degrees, everything fell into the regularity of subordination. With the subordination came increase of freedom. The steps of the more youthful of the family were heard on the stairs and in the corridors more light and quick than ever before. Their brother had lost the terrors of aspect produced by his confinement, and his commands were issued more gently, and oftener with a smile, than in all their previous history. By degrees his presence was universally felt through the house. It was no surprise to any one at his studies, to see him by his side when he lifted up his eyes, though he had not before known that he was in the room. And although some dread still remained, it was rapidly vanishing before the advances of a firm friendship. Without immediately ordering their labours, he always influenced them, and often altered their direction and objects. The change soon evident in the household was remarkable. A simpler, nobler expression was visible on all the countenances. The voices of the men were deeper, and yet seemed by their very depth more feminine than before; while the voices of the women were softer and sweeter, and at the same time more full and decided. Now the eyes had often an expression as if their sight was absorbed in the gaze of the inward eyes; and when the eyes of two met, there passed between those eyes the utterance of a conviction that both meant the same thing. But the change was, of course, to be seen more clearly, though not more evidently, in individuals.

One of the brothers, for instance, was very fond of astronomy. He had his observatory on a lofty tower, which stood pretty clear of the others, towards the north and east. But hitherto, his astronomy, as he had called it, had been more of the character of astrology. Often, too, he might have been seen directing a heaven-searching telescope to catch the rapid transit of a fiery shooting-star, belonging altogether to the earthly atmosphere, and not to the serene heavens. He had to learn that the signs of the air are not the signs of the skies. Nay, once, his brother surprised him in the act of examining through his longest tube a patch of burning heath upon a distant hill. But now he was diligent from morning till night in the study of the laws of the truth that has to do with stars; and when the curtain of the sun-light was about to rise from before the heavenly worlds which it had hidden all day long, he might be seen preparing his instruments with that solemn countenance with which it becometh one to look into the mysterious harmonies of nature. Now he learned what law and order and truth are, what consent and harmony mean; how the individual may find his own end in a higher end, where law and freedom mean the same thing, and the purest certainty exists without the slightest constraint. Thus he stood on the earth, and looked to the heavens.

167

Another, who had been much given to searching out the hollow places and recesses in the foundations of the castle, and who was often to be found with compass and ruler working away at a chart of the same which he had been in process of constructing, now came to the conclusion, that only by ascending the upper regions of his abode, could he become capable of understanding what lay beneath; and that, in all probability, one clear prospect, from the top of the highest attainable turret, over the castle as it lay below, would reveal more of the idea of its internal construction, than a year spent in wandering through its subterranean vaults. But the fact was, that the desire to ascend wakening within him had made him forget what was beneath; and having laid aside his chart for a time at least, he was now to be met in every quarter of the upper parts, searching and striving upward, now in one direction, now in another; and seeking, as he went, the best outlooks into the clear air of outer realities.

And they began to discover that they were all meditating different aspects of the same thing; and they brought together their various discoveries, and recognized the likeness between them; and the one thing often explained the other, and combining with it helped to a third. They grew in consequence more and more friendly and loving; so that every now and then, one turned to another and said, as in surprise, "Why, you are my brother!"—"Why, you are my sister!" And yet they had always known it.

The change reached to all. One, who lived on the air of sweet sounds, and who was almost always to be found seated by her harp or some other instrument, had, till the late storm, been generally merry and playful, though sometimes sad. But for a long time after that, she was often found weeping, and playing little simple airs which she had heard in childhood—backward longings, followed by fresh tears. Before long, however, a new element manifested itself in her music. It became yet more wild, and sometimes retained all its sadness, but it was mingled with anticipation and hope. The past and the future merged in one; and while memory yet brought the rain-cloud, expectation threw the rainbow across its bosom— and all was uttered in her music, which rose and swelled, now to defiance, now to victory; then died in a torrent of weeping.

As to the eldest sister, it was many days before she recovered from the shock. At length, one day, her brother came to her, took her by the hand, led her to an open window, and told her to seat herself by it, and look out. She did so; but at first saw nothing more than an unsympathizing blaze of sunlight. But as she looked, the horizon widened out, and the dome of the sky ascended, till the grandeur seized upon her soul, and she fell on her knees and wept. Now the heavens seemed to bend lovingly over her, and to stretch out wide cloud-arms to embrace her; the earth lay like the bosom of an infinite love beneath her, and the wind kissed her cheek with an odour of roses. She sprang to her feet, and turned, in an agony of hope, expecting to behold the face of the father, but there stood only her brother, looking calmly though lovingly on her emotion. She turned again to the window. On the hill-tops rested the sky: Heaven and Earth were one; and the prophecy awoke in her soul, that from betwixt them would the steps of the father approach.

Hitherto she had seen but beauty; now she beheld truth. Often had she looked on such clouds as these, and loved the strange ethereal curves into which the winds moulded them; and had smiled as her little pet sister told her what curious animals she saw in them, and tried to point them out to her. Now they were as

169

troops of angels, jubilant over her new birth, for they sang, in her soul, of beauty, and truth, and love. She looked down, and her little sister knelt beside her.

She was a curious child, with black, glittering eyes, and dark hair; at the mercy of every wandering wind; a frolicsome, daring girl, who laughed more than she smiled. She was generally in attendance on her sister, and was always finding and bringing her strange things. She never pulled a primrose, but she knew the haunts of all the orchis tribe, and brought from them bees and butterflies innumerable, as offerings to her sister. Curious moths and glow-worms were her greatest delight; and she loved the stars, because they were like the glow-worms. But the change had affected her too; for her sister saw that her eyes had lost their glittering look, and had become more liquid and transparent. And from that time she often observed that her gaiety was more gentle, her smile more frequent, her laugh less bell-like; and although she was as wild as ever, there was more elegance in her motions, and more music in her voice. And she clung to her sister with far greater fondness than before.

The land reposed in the embrace of the warm summer days. The clouds of heaven nestled around the towers of the castle; and the hearts of its inmates became conscious of a warm atmosphere—of a presence of love. They began to feel like the children of a household, when the mother is at home. Their faces and forms grew daily more and more beautiful, till they wondered as they gazed on each other. As they walked in the gardens of the castle, or in the country around, they were often visited, especially the eldest sister, by sounds that no one heard by themselves, issuing from woods and waters; and by forms of love that lightened out of flowers, and grass, and great rocks. Now and then the young children would come in with a slow, stately step, and, with great eyes that looked as if they would devour all the creation, say that they had met the father amongst the trees, and that he had kissed them; "And," added one of them once, "I grew so big!" But when others went out to look, they could see no one. And some said it must have been the brother, who grew more and more beautiful, and loving, and reverend, and who had lost all traces of hardness, so that they wondered they could ever have thought him stern and harsh. But the eldest sister held her peace, and looked up, and her eyes filled with tears. "Who can tell," thought she, "but the little children know more about it than we?"

Often, at sunrise, might be heard their hymn of praise to their unseen father, whom they felt to be near, though they saw him not. Some words thereof once reached my ear through the folds of the music in which they floated, as in an upward snow-storm of sweet sounds. And these are some of the words I heard—but there was much I seemed to hear, which I could not understand, and some things which I understood but cannot utter again.

"We thank thee that we have a father, and not a maker; that thou hast begotten us, and not moulded us as images of clay; that we have come forth of thy heart, and have not been fashioned by thy hands. It *must* be so. Only the heart of a father is able to create. We rejoice in it, and bless thee that we know it. We thank thee for thyself. Be what thou art—our root and life, our beginning and end, our all in all. Come home to us. Thou livest; therefore we live. In thy light we see. Thou art—that is all our song."

Thus they worship, and love, and wait. Their hope and expectation grow ever stronger and brighter, that one day, ere long, the father will show himself amongst them, and thenceforth dwell in his own house for evermore. What was once but an old legend has become the one desire of their hearts.

And the loftiest hope is the surest of being fulfilled.